MY FANGtastically EVIL VaMPiRE PET

SURVIVAL
OF THE
FURRIEST

MO O'HARA

ILLUSTRATED BY MAREK JAGUCKI

FEIWEL AND FRIENDS 🐾 NEW YORK

A Feiwel and Friends Book
An imprint of Macmillan Publishing Group, LLC
120 Broadway, New York, NY 10271

Our books may be purchased in bulk for promotional, educational, or business use. Please contact your local bookseller or the Macmillan Corporate and Premium Sales Department at (800) 221-7945 ext. 5442 or by email at MacmillanSpecialMarkets@macmillan.com.

Library of Congress Cataloging-in-Publication Data is available.

Book design by Michael Burroughs

Printed in the United States by LSC Communications, Harrisonburg, Virginia

Feiwel and Friends logo designed by Filomena Tuosto

ISBN 978-1-250-12818-8 (hardcover)

10 9 8 7 6 5 4 3 2 1

To my amazing husband, Guy.
You inspire me every day. xxx
—M.O.

To my bother Dan, king of allotments!
—M. J.

Evil Scientist Summer Camp is almost over! So, this is my last chance to show my epic evil awesomeness and to prove to everyone at Camp Mwhaaa-haa-ha-a-watha that I totally deserve the Evil Emperor of the Week crown. And I have the perfect evil plan to get it!

They just announced that the Evil Celebrity Judge for this week is Dr. Cyberbyte (the Evil Cybernetic Mega Millionaire Inventor). Which is cool on many levels. I mean, all the best Evil Scientists have "Dr." in their name, right, so that's cool, and being a mega millionaire is definitely cool. But what is epically cool is that he just gave an interview in Evil Scientist magazine about his plan to make sure every Evil Scientist has an evil sidekick pet! I'm totally ahead of the game with my fierce evil vampire pet Fang.

Fang and I are gonna impress Dr. Cyberbyte so much that he will actually award us two crowns: one giant golden pointy scary one for me and a tiny kitten-size one for Fang (probably with a strap 'cause she'd pull it off right away).

OK, people, bring on the final Evil Scientist Camp Challenge!! Fang and I are gonna kick some cyber-butt!!

Mwhaaa-haa-haaa-ha-ha,

The Great and Powerful Mark

1

This morning I woke up with a kitten's backside on my face and her claws digging into my chest. Just for the record, this is not a great way to wake up.

"Get off!" I yelled. Then I remembered where I was. I couldn't let Diablo and Bob, my tentmates, see Fang, so I pretended I was just yawning really loud. "Awwwwwwwhhh," I fake yawned.

I whispered, "Fang, get off me!" and gently pried her claws off my T-shirt as I sat up in my bunk.

The noise of my shout must have woken Igor. He's a light sleeper.

"Urgh, urgh, urgh?" he mumbled sleepily and scratched his bald head.

"It's Fang," I whispered. "Something freaked her out. Maybe we should check?"

I got up, slipped on my sneakers, put on my white evil-scientist coat and headed to the front of the tent. Igor pulled a ski hat over his head and followed, looking like a sleepwalking mountain. He's a big guy. Fang leaped into the pocket of my coat as we left the tent.

It was only five a.m. and it was just starting to get light out there, but as soon as we looked outside, we could tell why Fang's danger sense had kicked in. Shadows were moving around by the other tents. People in what looked like hazmat suits like you would wear to avoid contamination or something were spraying the area around the tents.

"Urgh, urgh urgh urgh?" Igor whispered.

"Good plan." I nodded. "You go that way and I'll go this way."

As we panned out around the circle of tents, I overheard a couple of the people in suits talking.

"We've sprayed the outside perimeter. He's not going in any of the tents, so we don't have to worry about those," said one of them.

"Paranoid, if you ask me," the other guy said.

"When you're that rich you can be that paranoid too," the first guy added.

That's when we saw Geeky Girl come out of a tent across the clearing.

"Hey, do you have permission to do that?" Geeky Girl shouted into a megaphone.

A very tired-looking kid who usually woke us in the morning with the megaphone (or the bugle) followed her out of the tent, saying, "Can I have my megaphone back now, please?"

"No!" Geeky Girl said into the megaphone, then winced and lowered it. "Um, sorry," she said to the kid next to her, this time without the megaphone, "I'm still using it."

She lifted the megaphone and turned back to the hazmat guys. "You are on private Camp Mwhaaa-haa-ha-a-watha land and you should cease and desist!" she shouted again.

Fang stirred in my pocket like she was getting ready to pounce. I held her down.

"What?" the first guy in the hazmat suit shouted back.

Ezmirelda stepped up with Lucky, her guard Komodo dragon, at her side. He was licking his mouth in that "Oooh, I'm a little hungry for trespassers" kinda way.

"She means GO NOW." She paused. "My dragon is lookin' kinda hungry."

"We're done anyway," the second guy said and they ran off toward a van that was parked by the front entrance.

Geeky Girl gave the kid his megaphone back and ran over to Igor and me. Ezmirelda stomped over with Lucky.

"Well, that was a weird way to start the day?" I said as Fang climbed up my coat and onto my shoulder.

"Urgh, urgh, urgh, urgh?" Igor said.

"I don't know who they were but they were saying that 'he was paranoid' and 'if you're that rich you can be that paranoid too,'" I said.

"Wait, Dr. Cyberbyte is due this morning, right?" Geeky Girl said.

"Urgh," Igor answered.

"Dr. Cyberbyte is a complete germophobe. I've heard that he once decontaminated an entire fifty-story building before he would stop to use the bathroom," Geeky Girl said.

"And since when are you all up on the Evil Scientist gossip?" I said.

"I'm not," she said. "I just like to research who's coming to camp so I don't get surprised like last time."

"Urgh, urgh, urgh," Igor said.

"No, I don't have any more famous Evil

Scientists in my family," she said. "One is definitely enough. But I think this week could be challenging, finally, from a tech point of view. Dr. Cyberbyte might give us a global programming problem or we might work with cutting-edge AI?"

"Wow, you have been looking up Cyberbyte," I said. "Hey, I'm all for an epic challenge but not this early."

"Urgh, urgh, urgh," Igor agreed.

"Yeah, me too. I want to still be asleep," I said.

"And not woken by some weirdos in space suits spraying the camp," Ezmirelda grumbled and stomped off again.

"Urgh, urgh, urgh," Igor said.

"Yeah, she's not a morning person." I nodded and we turned to head toward the mess tent to get a snack. "You want some breakfast, Fang?" She jumped into my pocket again and licked her mouth.

"OK, he may be paranoid about germs and stuff, but Dr. Cyberbyte is still going to be a completely epic evil judge of the week," I said.

"He's certainly successful," Geeky Girl said. "He has so many computer patents and programs that he created. The man is a genius."

"Urgh, urgh," Igor added.

"Correct," I said. "Evil genius."

"Oh, somebody is talking about me," we heard Sanj say behind us.

2

"You wish," Geeky Girl said, turning around
to face Sanj. "There's a slight difference between
being able to hack your school computer and
inventing a program that spaghettifies all your
data into a number tornado and then
wrecks your hard drive."

"That was just lucky,"
Sanj said. "I could do
that. I only need time
and investment to be a
perfect evil computer
genius. When I win
the competition this
week, Dr. Cyberbyte will
undoubtedly invest in my

future at his company." Sanj smiled. "It takes a true evil genius to recognize another true evil genius."

"Urgh." Igor nodded.

"Yeah, shame no one has recognized your genius yet, Sanj," I added.

"It is, but he soon will. I have the skills to impress Dr. Cyberbyte. I have the ambition. I just need the perfect project to pitch to him," Sanj said, typing away on his tablet. "I'm working on several evil ideas. I think it's fair to say that I have this week's challenge in the bag."

"I wouldn't count on it," I said. "Geeky Girl is pretty epic with the computer stuff. Even if it's not evil. She might blow your ideas out of the water."

"Urgh, urgh, urgh," Igor said.

"Yeah, like a tornado!" I agreed and high-fived Igor.

"Actually, I have developed a hack to Dr. Cyberbyte's tornado data app to make it into a tsunami that can crash into someone else's hard drive from a phone on Bluetooth," Geeky Girl said.

"But his apps are unhackable," Sanj said.

"Not if you give it a Trojan horse." Geeky Girl smiled.

"I'm just gonna say it because I know you're thinking it too, Igor. Why would an app want a horse?" I said.

"You hide malware in something that the app wants or needs to download. Like it's a gift. You remember from ancient history? The Trojan wars? The Trojan horse?" Geeky Gill looked at Igor and me.

"Nope, I think I slept through that bit of history class. I slept through most bits of history class. Now if they did evil history . . ."

Geeky Girl interrupted. "This is kinda evil history. Or at least sneaky history. So, the app lets you in because you are disguised as something it wants."

"And then it catches you when you least expect it," Sanj added, still typing away on his tablet. "Like I could Bluetooth a command from my tablet that is pretending to be, say, an amusing GIF from Mark's phone so your software wouldn't block it. Then once it was in it would steal your blueprint for your tsunami hack." Sanj was doing a truly creepy smile. "You have potential, Geeky Girl, but you definitely lack any much-needed evil intent."

Geeky Girl looked down at her tablet, which was scrolling through screens and appearing to be sending off files. She scrambled to click buttons and it stopped. "My plans!" she mumbled.

"My plans now," Sanj said. "Don't worry, I'll improve them. I saw some things I could tweak already."

The tablet whirred to a stop. Geeky Girl glared at Sanj. "You can't use that! It's my work."

"All's fair in war and cyber-pirating." Sanj laughed his totally wheezy laugh.

"You give it back to her now," I said and stepped toward Sanj. Fang was growling in my pocket, ready to pounce.

"Give her back what?" Sanj gave an innocent look.

I grabbed the tablet from him.

"There's nothing on it. All in the cloud." He smiled but pulled back, knowing that if I wanted to, I could easily decide to smash his tablet or his face.

"He's not worth it," Geeky Girl said. "You can't risk being kicked out right before the end of camp."

I tossed the tablet back to him. "You are lucky," I said to Sanj.

"No, I'm smart," Sanj added. "Once Dr. Cyberbyte sees my improved tsunami plans, he'll definitely take me on."

Then Sanj swanned off.

"OH!!!! I walked right into that!!" Geeky Girl kicked her sneaker in the dirt. "I let him take it!"

"He used the same sneaky pony thing that you were talking about on you?" I asked.

"Not sneaky pony! Trojan horse!!!" she shouted. Then she seemed to calm down super quick.

"Two can play at that game. OK, he may have my plans but there is no way Sanj is winning this week's challenge. I am going to impress Dr. Cyberbyte with something so new, so cutting-edge, so full-on computer genius that I have to win."

"You can think up something ten times better," I said. "And no way any of us are gonna let Sanj win this thing. Spooky donkey or not."

"Urgh, urgh!" Igor corrected.

"Right, Trojan horse. Right," I added. "Anyway, I think Dr. Cyberbyte is looking for more than computer skills anyway."

"What do you mean?" Geeky Girl asked.

"I like Dr. Cyberbyte not because of his whole being-an-epically-successful-evil-genius thing and not even because of the very cool computer tornado app," I said as I pulled a folded-up page from *Evil Scientist* magazine out of my pocket. "It's this."

"Every Evil Scientist Needs an Evil Sidekick Pet," Geeky Girl read the headline out loud and then started to scan the article.

"You see? This is gonna be the week where I can literally let the cat out of the bag. Or let the kitten out of my evil-scientist coat pocket." I stroked Fang behind the ears while Geeky Girl and Igor looked over the newspaper clipping.

You see, I had planned it all out. Dr. Cyberbyte thought that every Evil Scientist should have his own pet, so I would introduce him to Fang. He would see how cool it is that she is pocket-size evil and that she is the perfect evil sidekick. And maybe if he likes that I have Fang then Geeky Girl will step up and say that she has Boris (even if he is technically not an EVIL sidekick pet, just a boring old ordinary sidekick pet) and Ezmirelda will step up and say that she has Lucky as an actual pet and not just a guard Komodo dragon for the camp like she agreed so that the dragon wouldn't bite any of the counselors. That was the plan anyway.

Geeky Girl looked up from the article. "I get it. I mean, you need Fang and I need Boris," she said, "but is Dr. Cyberbyte really that into evil pets?"

"That's what it says." I took back the piece of paper and read from the article, "An Evil Scientist without an evil pet is like a bike without a wheel, like a computer without a chip . . ."

Igor interrupted, "Urgh urgh, urgh urgh urgh, urgh urgh urgh urgh."

"Exactly! Like a peanut butter cookie without the peanut butter!" I agreed and went to high-five Igor but he looked down.

Then it hit me. I had Fang. Geeky Girl had Boris. Igor was a cookie without his peanut butter.

3

I changed the subject fast. "He is probably going to come up with some completely epic challenge for this week and we are ready for him, aren't we?"

"Urgh." Igor nodded.

"No matter what. I am ready to take down Sanj," Geeky Girl growled. Fang purred almost like she was impressed with the underlying evil twang in Geeky Girl's words.

"That calls for some toast, I think," I said as we hit the mess tent.

"What are you doing out of your tents?" I heard the voice through the megaphone behind us.

We turned around to see Kirsty Katastrophe, evil cheerleader and terrifying yet perky camp counselor, standing on top of the kid with the megaphone and shouting at us. That kid was having a worse morning than us.

"We were just making sure that the guys who were detoxing the camp were gone," I shouted back.

She jumped down off the kid's shoulders and strode toward us.

"Dr. Cyberbyte might have some different ideas of how to prepare for his trip to Camp Mwhaaa-haa-ha-a-watha, but whatever Dr. Cyberbyte wants Dr. Cyberbyte gets. He is beyond important in Evil Science circles and nothing is going to mess up this week," she said as she leaned in toward us. "Nothing. Got it?"

"We got it," I said.

"Urgh, urgh, urgh," Igor echoed.

"I was just thinking maybe we could—" Geeky Girl started to say but Kirsty cut her off.

"Got it?" She leaned in a bit more menacingly. "NOTHING will mess up this week."

"Yeah, got it," Geeky Girl said.

"Good," Kirsty answered. "Now get back to your tents and get ready. Dr. Cyberbyte is starting very early. He likes to wake with the sun."

"I like to wake with some toast," I mumbled.

"Wait, before you get any breakfast, I have a job for you all since you are the first campers up and about," Kirsty commanded.

"To do what?" Geeky Girl said.

"You can all go down to the front gate and make sure that the road coming in is clear. We've had reports of tires punctured this week in the driveway, so we want to make sure there

are no stones or sharp rocks that could damage Dr. Cyberbyte's transport. Everything has to be perfect."

She handed us all rakes and sent us down the drive to the front gate.

"When you are done you can head back to your tents and don't come out until you get the signal," Kirsty shouted after us.

"Urgh, urgh, urgh?" Igor asked.

"What?" Kirsty looked at Igor.

"What's the signal?" Geeky Girl said.

"You'll know." She smiled.

We took our rakes down to the front gate, where

the guardhouse was. Ez patrols the entrance with Lucky sometimes when she's bored. But she was tucked up back in her bunk by now, so there was no sound of a stomping snarling Komodo dragon to interrupt the birdsong and the wind in the trees. Then my stomach rumbled.

"OK, let's get this over so we can eat. My stomach was tricked into getting up early and now it's seriously mad that I haven't fed it yet," I said, practically shouting over the stomach growl.

Igor pulled his hat down over his ears and mumbled, "Urgh, urgh, urgh."

"It is too chilly to be out of bed," I agreed, "especially without breakfast."

Fang jumped out of my pocket and started sniffing the ground. Then she suddenly stopped and jumped into attack cat stance. "What's up, Fang? Do you sense something else down here?"

Just then Boris, Geeky Girl's non-evil sidekick pet budgie, fluttered onto her shoulder from a nearby tree.

"Urgh, urgh, urgh," Igor said.

"Yeah, I guess her budgie sensors were on there," I said.

But Fang didn't relax when Boris landed. Instead she meowed and pointed with her paw, and Boris flew over to where she was pointing.

"What are they up to?" Geeky Girl said, already raking the area to get rid of rocks and stones.

"Maybe it's a game?" I said.

Boris landed on the gate that lifts up to let people into the camp. It was still closed, so it stretched across the driveway. Boris tweeted.

"I think Boris has seen something," Geeky Girl said.

She went up to get a closer look. That's when the rock moved.

A gray-brown rock, about the size of my fist, rolled really fast toward Geeky Girl.

She jumped back and Boris flapped off the gate and landed on her shoulder again.

Fang pounced into action. She arched her back Halloween-cat style and sidestepped toward the moving rock, hissing as she went.

"Hssssssss," the rock hissed back.

"Urgh, urgh, urgh?" Igor said.

"Fang, stay back!" I shouted. "What is that thing? Is this a trick? Are we on some Internet prank show or something?" I looked around for cameras. "A moving, hissing rock?"

"It's an animal, I think," Geeky Girl said. "Maybe that's what's been puncturing the tires of vehicles coming into camp?"

"Whatever it is it doesn't sound happy to see us, or especially Fang," I added.

Just then the rock rolled toward Fang and Fang pounced back. There was a blur of gray fur and jagged edges as they kicked up the dirt in the road. A cloud of dirt swirled around them.

Then we heard a whirring sound and then a rumbling.

"Something is coming up the road," I said.

It was a convoy of black vehicles with darkened windows pulling trailers all loaded with crates. They were headed toward the camp gates.

Fang and whatever she was fighting were directly under the gates.

Igor shouted, "URGH! URGH!"

The bar lifted automatically as the cars approached.

I waved to get them to stop.

"They are headed right for Fang!" I shouted.

"It's OK, Mark!" Geeky Girl shouted. "They are hover cars!"

Looking again, as the vehicles got up to the gate, I could see that there were no tires on any of the cars.

The lead car slowed and a man with a styled mop of whitish-gray hair and a turtleneck leaned out the window.

"Dr. Cyberbyte?" I mumbled. "Wow."

"Yeah, I get that a lot." (He paused and adjusted his hair.) "I presume this is Camp Mwhaaa-haa-ha-a-watha?" He smiled. "Are you the welcome escorts to take us to the camp? Charming." He smiled again and then turned to the hazmat guys who were in the backseat. "Spray them."

They leaned out the window and sprayed the disinfectant over Geeky Girl, Igor, and me.

We all spluttered and stumbled back.

"We'll see you up at the campsite. Don't be late," Dr. Cyberbyte added from inside the car.

"Wait! Fang!" I tried to shout, but it came out as a cough and a grunt.

The hover car moved forward, and just as it hit the cloud of dust from Fang and whatever she was fighting with, the hover car bucked up and jumped like something had kicked it from underneath. I saw Fang leap out from the cloud of dust and dive behind a shrub as a few crates fell off the back of the trailer.

At least she was OK. And still hidden from view for now.

"What was that?" Dr. Cyberbyte asked. "The hover cars have pretty solid stabilizers. What could have done that?"

"Urgh, urgh urgh?" Igor offered.

"He says there are some pretty big rocks in the road," Geeky Girl translated. "We were just clearing them for your arrival. We weren't completely done, I guess," she added.

Dr. Cyberbyte motioned for the convoy to drive on. "I guess you better finish, then," he said and waved as they pulled away.

"Urgh, urgh!" Igor shouted after the cars.

"Yeah, you dropped some boxes!" Geeky Girl translated, but the cars were already too far ahead to hear.

I ran to the shrub and scooped up Fang. "Are you OK, kitten?"

She purred and licked my hand.

"What was that little thing?" I said, looking over at Igor and Geeky Girl.

"I don't know but whatever it was it had a darn good kick," Geeky Girl said. "It knocked that hover car three feet in the air!"

"Urgh, urgh, urgh," Igor said, looking around.

"Whatever it was, it's rolled away for now. I guess we know what's been puncturing tires for

the last couple weeks," I said. "Come on, let's head back to camp. I don't want to miss anything Dr. Cyberbyte says."

As we walked back up the driveway I mumbled to myself, "I can't believe Dr. Cyberbyte spoke to me first. Out of everyone in the camp. It was fate."

"I think it was more like you were standing in the way of his car, so he had to talk to you," Geeky Girl said.

"Yeah, but that's still fate," I said and stroked Fang as I slid her into my pocket again as we got to camp. Boris fluttered off GG's shoulder and into another tree.

As we got to the tents, we heard the megaphone/bugle kid playing his morning bugle call to wake up the campers. "Brahhp, braaaap, braaap, braaaaaaaa, braaaaaaaaaap."

"Urgh urgh?" Igor said.

"I think you're right," I said. "I think he's playing 'My Way.'"

I turned to Geeky Girl. "My gran likes that song," I said. "She's a Sinatra fan."

"Yeah, my grandma likes it too," Geeky Girl said. "But for her it's probably for more big evil ego reasons, being a famously ruthless Evil Scientist and all. Still, she's my grandma."

We stood back on the edge of the camp by the tents while the rest of the campers all gathered in the center area where Kirsty and Phillipe Fortescue, master of evil disguise, were waiting on the stage.

5

Igor was still looking pretty glum. I felt bad about mentioning the whole needing-an-evil-sidekick-pet thing in front of him. We'd need to distract him with a good evil plan this week. That should take his mind off it.

We'll make sure Sanj doesn't win the challenge with his stolen plans and we'll impress Dr. Cyberbyte with our inventions and our fantastically evil sidekick pets.

Then we will make history by having the first pets at Camp Mwhaaa-haa-ha-a-watha, and from then on we can tear up the no-pets rule forever!!

My daydream of total evil-pet freedom was interrupted by Igor tapping me on the shoulder.

"Owww," I said. Igor tends to tap pretty hard.

I turned to where he was pointing. The hazmat suit guys were back and they were laying out a red carpet to the clearing in front of the stage. The convoy of black hover cars with dark windows were parked just by the stage. Dr. Cyberbyte must still be inside.

Ezmirelda stomped over to us with Lucky on his chain. Lucky was pulling toward the cars and hissing. He did not look happy. And not just his normal "I could eat you all as soon as look at you" not happy, but more of an "I'm going to eat you first because I don't trust you as far as I could fling

you with my tail, which is pretty darn far" kind of
not happy.

"I don't think Lucky likes this guy," Ezmirelda
said.

"And he's not even out of his car yet," I added.

Kirsty Katastrophe looked over at Igor, Geeky
Girl, Ezmirelda and me and shot us a look that
pretty much said "Don't mess this up!!!" We all
understood the look.

Then Trevor came up to us. "Zere is a job for you. Dr. Cyberbyte needs someone to get zee boxes zat fell off zee trailer," he said. "Ve ezpezially need you," he said as he pointed to Igor. "Zey are pretty heavy he says."

"Urgh, urgh, urgh." Igor shrugged.

"Dr. Cyberbyte needs all the boxes for his talk to zee campers," Trevor ordered. "Bring zem up here right avay."

"Great," I said and we all headed off to pick up the metal boxes from the drive. "We get to be the henchmen again."

"Hench people," Ezmirelda growled. "And what boxes?"

"There's some little animal thing down by the front gate," I said. "It knocked boxes off the trailers as they drove in."

"OK, Lucky, maybe that's a snack for you, then," Ez said.

"I'm sick of people thinking we're just henchmen . . . Hench people, whatever," I said. "I want Dr. Cyberbyte to see me as an Evil Scientist that he can work with and that totally deserves to be Evil Emperor of the Week."

"I just want to think up an invention that's better than the tsunami app that Sanj stole," Geeky Girl added.

When we were down the drive and around the corner, Boris landed again on Geeky Girl's shoulder.

Fang jumped out of my pocket and meowed at Boris. Lucky hissed at them both. Ya know, it was like a normal sidekick-pet reunion, really.

We all started walking toward fallen boxes by a ditch by the driveway when Fang took off toward the ditch.

"Not again, no, Fang!" I shouted at her.

Her fur was on end and she was back doing that "Halloween cat" thing where they arch their back and point their tails straight up. Lucky was tasting the air with his tongue, and you could tell something didn't taste right.

Just as we all peered over the side of the ditch, Fang leaped out again. "Reoooooowwwlll!" she meowed.

We looked down to see a tight ball of fur and spikes. Fang jumped into my arms. A single spike stuck out of her backside. I gently tugged it free.

"Ouch, kitten. That must hurt," I said. "But you should know not to pick fights with ..." I paused. "... with whatever that little spiky thing is."

Lucky flicked his tongue toward the spiky ball and it shot out a quill so fast that it hit Lucky's tongue.

"Hisssss," he protested with a very mopey hiss.

Boris stayed away. He was not a stupid budgie. He wasn't taking any chances.

"Urgh, urgh, urgh, urgh," Igor said.

"I think you're right," Geeky Girl answered. "It's a hedgehog. But hedgehogs can't shoot spikes like that?"

"Urgh, urgh, urgh," Igor said.

"No one told that to this hedgehog, I guess," I translated.

Igor got down on his knees and started to reach out to the spiky ball. He took off his ski hat and held it out to the creature like a little wool nest.

"You'll get spiked," I said. "That little thing is fierce. You saw what it did to Cyberbyte's car."

But when Igor held out his hand the little spiky ball started to unroll itself. It looked up at Igor and for the first time we could see its face. This hedgehog had a monobrow. It was like a little prickly, round Igor.

"Urgh, urgh, urgh, urgh, urgh," Igor said and gently scooped up the hedgehog in the hat and lifted him out of the ditch.

"OK, I'm not good at translating Igor's urghs yet," Ezmirelda said. "But did he just say, 'I found my peanut butter'?"

Geeky Girl and I nodded. "That's exactly what he said," I answered.

"Um . . . Igor," Geeky Girl started to say, "this is a little wild animal. I don't know if he'll want to be an evil sidekick pet. Or even if he likes . . ." But then she stopped.

The hedgehog had snuffled up onto Igor's shoulder and was staring at Igor's monobrow.

"Vhy are you taking so long?!" Trevor shouted from around the corner.

6

In a second the hedgehog had leaped up onto
Igor's head, tucked in and curled around like a
spiky hedgehog Mohawk of hair. Boris flew off to a
branch and Fang jumped back into my pocket.

When Trevor rounded the corner and saw us
by the ditch, we all pretended that everything was
completely normal.

"Grab zose boxes and get moving. Dr.
Cyberbyte is about to start," Trevor said. We all
rushed to pick up the boxes. Then Trevor stopped,
turned and looked at Igor.

"You done something different vith your hair?"
he said.

"Urgh, urgh, urgh," Igor said nervously.

"Yeah, he's trying out a new evil-henchman . . .

I mean evil-hench-person look,"
I added.

"I think it's menacing,"
Ezmirelda said.

"I agree," said Trevor.
"Now, move it."

Igor carried a box himself
and the rest of us all carried
the other one and followed
Trevor back to the stage area.

Igor got a few nods from
other campers as we passed.

"I like the new look," Dustin said to Igor. "I
can recommend a cream for those split ends," he
added.

"Just keep walking," I whispered to Igor.
"Nobody has noticed the hedgehog, so we'll just go
with it."

We put the boxes onstage and then went off to
the side to join the crowd.

Trevor nodded toward the cars.

There was a collective gasp from the whole crowd as the front car door opened and out stepped Dr. Cyberbyte. He was super cool-looking with his whitish-gray hair and dark glasses, skinny pants and dark turtleneck top. "Hey, young evil dudes and dudettes," he said and brushed his hand through his hair and finished it in a wave.

"Nice hair," Dustin mumbled, stroking his own tumbling locks. "Respect."

A cheer erupted from the group as he took off his dark glasses and winked at the crowd. Then he motioned to the hazmat guys and they sprayed the crowd with some kind of anti-germ spray.

The group cheer turned into more of a group cough and splutter from being sprayed.

Man, this guy really did think we were plague carriers or something. I covered Fang's face as she peeked out of my coat pocket. Igor covered his head but not before a tiny sneeze came from the Mohawk. "Achoo."

Diablo and Bob looked over at Igor.

"I know," I said. "For such a big guy he has a really delicate sneeze, doesn't he?" I elbowed Igor and he made a very tiny "achoo" noise.

Then Dr. Cyberbyte stepped onto a small hoverboard that the guys in the hazmat suits placed at his feet. It glided along the red carpet, carrying him through the crowd of confused coughing-but-still-trying-to-cheer campers.

When he got to the front, he jumped off the hoverboard, heel-kicked it up in the air, caught it and then handed it off to one of the hazmat guys and stepped up to the microphone. The guy was just scientifically distilled evil coolness. Respect. Trevor, Phillipe and Kirsty all stood next to him. They all looked like they were trying to be as effortlessly cool as he was, but they just weren't cutting it.

"Thank you, Dr. Cyberbyte," Phillipe said. "We are extremely excited to have you as our Evil Celebrity Judge for this week's challenge."

"Thanks so much," Dr. Cyberbyte said. "And I have brought a surprise along to the camp. I hope you like it."

Dr. Cyberbyte grinned as two of the hazmat guys brought forward one of the metal boxes.

"Some of you may know that I'm a bit of a trendsetter in the world of Evil Science," Dr. Cyberbyte said as he walked around the side of the large box.

"I don't follow other people's ideas. I think up my own. And then I usually make millions of dollars from selling that idea to somebody else." He smiled, obviously thinking about the piles of money that must sit around in his mansion and need to be dusted by all his minions on a regular basis.

"Recently my thoughts have turned to evil sidekicks." He paused and looked around at the campers.

This was it.

"I was quoted in *Evil Scientist* magazine recently as saying, 'Every Evil Scientist needs an evil sidekick pet.'"

There were mumbles from the crowd and even a tut-tut noise from over where the camp counselors stood.

"Or even a non-evil sidekick pet," Geeky Girl mumbled to me.

"I stand by that statement; every Evil Scientist needs an evil sidekick pet. In order to be a truly effective Evil Scientist, you need to maximize your time and effort, and the right evil sidekick pet can help you in ways you can't yet imagine," he said.

He looked over at us and then momentarily paused when he spotted Igor's "hair." He pushed his own whitish-gray quiff back off his forehead, gave Igor a thumbs-up and then continued.

"So evil sidekick pets are essential," he added. "But not just ANY evil sidekick pet."

"Yeah, well, obviously," I agreed and nudged Geeky Girl. "Fang is not just ANY sidekick pet. Are you, girl?"

Fang purred slightly as I scratched her behind the ear while she curled up in my coat pocket.

I almost stepped forward to show Dr. Cyberbyte my perfect evil sidekick pet. He would love Fang.

But then he started talking again, so I waited.

"That is why I have not left your choice of evil sidekick pet to chance. I, Dr. Cyberbyte, have created, using artificial intelligence, the perfect evil sidekick pet."

Fang stopped purring immediately and her fur stood on end.

"Behold." Dr. Cyberbyte lifted his arm over the metal box. "Cyber-dog 5000."

The sides of the metal box dropped down to reveal what looked like a robot dog standing there onstage. Its eyes were bright green and it pivoted its head like it was taking in its surroundings. Kinda like it was scanning us all.

7

I stepped back with the others.

Lucky was pulling at his chain, trying to get to the cyber dog. Igor had to help Ez hold him back.

"The Cyber-dog 5000 is far superior to a real pet in so many ways. It is programmed to do what you want it to do. No mistakes." Dr. Cyberbyte patted his leg and the dog walked to him and sat down by his side.

"No accidentally chewing the cords on your latest evil invention," he said.

I looked down at Fang and she looked away guiltily.

"No biting the delivery person when they bring you your new laser ray that you ordered online."

Ez looked over at Lucky, who did not look at all

guilty. In fact, he licked his lips.

"No pooping on the windshield of the getaway car," he added.

Boris took this opportunity to fly overhead and drop a bird poop right on the head of the Cyber-dog 5000.

Geeky Girl rolled her eyes and smiled. "OK, so maybe Boris is a tiny bit evil."

The guys in the hazmat suits stepped up to the cyber dog and sprayed him with some of the decontaminant spray and cleaned off the Boris poop.

Then Dr. Cyberbyte continued. "But the main advantage of the Cyber-dog 5000 is that neither you nor the pet will develop any emotional attachments that might make one weak and not properly evil when one needs to be."

Fang clawed her way to the top of my pocket

but I held her down so she couldn't jump out at Dr. Cyberbyte and the cyber dog.

"We are going to give this next generation of Evil Scientists the advantage of a lifetime." Dr. Cyberbyte smiled.

Suddenly all the boxes' sides dropped down to reveal lots of identical Cyber-dog 5000s.

"Every kid in the camp is going to be issued a Cyber-dog 5000."

We stared at all the Cyber-dog 5000s.

"The dogs have fantastic AI systems in their positronic brains," Dr. Cyberbyte said as he tapped the metal dog on its head. "They can learn and figure things out from what they have been taught before.

"Innate in their programming are the three basic rules of Evil Robotics:

One: The Cyber-dog 5000 must not let their master come to any harm.

Two: The Cyber-dog 5000 must follow the orders of their master unless those orders conflict with rule one.

Three: The Cyber-dog 5000 must protect its own existence unless it conflicts with rule one or rule two.

"What is great about these cyber dogs is that they never need feeding, they never get tired and they never need any of that unnecessary petting, scratching and playing fetch that real dogs seem to need."

Bob yelled out, "Yeah and a metal pet isn't gonna make me sneeze."

"That is a definite advantage," Dr. Cyberbyte replied. "I hate sneezing," he added.

"The best bit is that these Cyber-dog 5000s just keep going and never give up. Until their batteries need a recharge, that is." He laughed.

Kirsty Katastrophe stepped forward. "Each camper will be assigned a dog."

Geeky Girl started to raise her hand. Kirsty glared at her and said, "No questions. This is mandatory, people. You have to take the dog."

Then Phillipe stepped forward too. "Each dog has been programmed to follow your commands once you voice-imprint on the dog. We'll then have a training session on how to best use your Cyber-dog 5000."

Trevor walked to the microphone and said, "And zee camper who comes up vith zee most ingenious vay of showing zee amazing usefulness of zee cyber dog vill vin zee Emperor of zee Veek crown."

Dr. Cyberbyte clapped his hands and each dog starting walking toward one kid in the camp. When they got to their person, they sat down next to them.

"I'll just activate the cyber dogs' trackers and sensors now. And they are ready to go," Dr. Cyberbyte said as he pressed some buttons on his tablet.

Just then the four cyber dogs that were standing by Geeky Girl, Ez, Igor and I started beeping.

"Ummmm. I think maybe we got some dud dogs over here," I said, stepping back from the beeping dogs.

"Nonsense. There are no 'dud' dogs. It seems as though their pet sensors have detected a pet in the vicinity," Dr. Cyberbyte said, looking at readings on his tablet.

"There are no pets in Camp Mwhaaa-haa-ha-a-watha," Kirsty said.

"Right!" said Geeky Girl and me at the same time. Not at all suspiciously.

"What do you call that, then?" Dr. Cyberbyte said, pointing at Lucky.

"Urgh, urgh, urgh," Igor answered.

"A what?"

Ez replied, "Lucky is not a pet. He is a guard

dragon." She paused. "And he doesn't seem to like the dogs any more than they like him." Lucky was hissing at the dogs as they beeped back.

"Well, he's setting off their sensors. We'll have to have Lucky outside the camp perimeter for the Cyber-dog 5000s to function properly. Otherwise the sensors going off will be a distraction."

Phillipe stepped forward. "Perhaps the dragon could reside in the guard shed at the end of the drive this week? So, the dogs aren't put off."

He started to reach for the chain to lead Lucky away but Lucky snapped at him. "Maybe you should take him yourself," he said to Ez.

I looked over at GG and Igor. "We should help Ez. You know, just in case," I said. "She might need Igor to . . . to . . . lift Lucky maybe?"

"Why on earth would I need to lift Lucky . . . ," Ez started to growl at me and then saw my look of "We need to get our pets out of here too because if you leave with Lucky and the pet alarms are still going off they'll look in my pocket and on Igor's head and we'll be done for."

Granted, it was a complicated look. But I think she got some of it.

"Yeah, right. I might need to lift the dragon," she muttered. And we all headed off toward the shed.

Our dogs started to follow us. "Stay," Geeky Girl commanded the dogs.

"Stay," I repeated, trying to copy the "pay attention to me, dog" tone in Geeky Girl's voice. I think I nailed it first time. The dog stopped in its tracks.

"Urgh," said Igor.

"Don't even think about it," said Ez.

All the cyber dogs obeyed us and stayed. It was pretty cool.

"We'll be right back," I said.

As we walked down the drive and turned the corner I whispered to Fang, "How come you never do what I ask like that?" All I got in response was a scratch and a meow.

8

Once we got to the shed Boris flew down and landed on Geeky Girl's shoulder again, and the little hedgehog unrolled and jumped off Igor's head.

"We have to leave all the pets here. It's not safe for them up at camp with all the cyber dogs around," I said.

"Urgh, urgh, urgh?" Igor asked.

"I don't know what the dogs would do if they caught a pet and I don't really want to find out," I answered.

We locked up Lucky in the shed and left the other pets free around the shed but told them not to come back to camp. It wasn't safe.

"They're going to be missing us," Geeky Girl said, ruffling Boris's top feathers. "We need to go."

I scratched Fang on the tummy and stood up. "OK, stay outta camp and stay away from Lucky." And then I whispered, "And you remember what happened with the hedgehog too."

Igor put the hedgehog down and he curled up into a little ball by the shed wall.

"Urgh, urgh, urgh, urgh," Igor said and patted the tiny spiky head.

"Aww, I think that's a good name for him," Geeky Girl said.

"Urgh, urgh, urgh?" Igor asked.

"Nah," Ez said, "it's a good evil name. It's like

a trick name. You think the pet is going to be sweet and then *Boing!* You are stuck with spikes from the fierce little thing."

"Peanut Butter it is, then," I said. "Bye, Fang. Don't mess with Peanut Butter, or Boris or Lucky."

Fang rolled her eyes and then rolled on the ground to show that she completely wasn't listening to me.

"OK, let's go," I said. "I wanna see what these cyber dogs can do."

🐾 🐾 🐾

When we got back to camp the other campers had already started working with their cyber dogs.

And our dogs were sitting there waiting for us right where we left them.

"Heel," Geeky Girl shouted and the dog bounded over to her and walked beside her.

When Igor and I called to ours they came right over too.

"It is kinda cool to have a robot pet that does what you want, isn't it?" I said to Igor.

"Urgh, urgh urgh urgh," Igor responded.

"Right," I agreed. "Not if it tries to eat Peanut Butter."

"Oh, the dogs won't try to eat your peanut butter sandwich like a normal dog might!" Dr. Cyberbyte was suddenly standing behind us. "That's another great thing about these pets. They don't steal food."

"Um, sure, right, um . . . Right, of course not," I said.

I had so much to say to this man and all I could manage was "um" and "right."

"You better get started. Your fellow campers are already programming their Cyber-dog 5000s with specialist skills. So, did you get rid of the dragon?"

Ez started to bristle more than an angry hedgehog. "We put him in the guard shed at the camp entrance," she said.

"Good," Dr. Cyberbyte said. "We can't have any interference from live animals."

Then he looked over at Igor. "You changed your hair?"

"Urgh, urgh," Igor said and mimed shaving his head.

"Shame, it looked menacing," he said.

"That's what I said," Ez agreed.

"Good luck with your cyber dogs," he said, and walked away to see some of the other campers' work.

We looked around at what everyone else was doing.

Diablo had a cool plan for teaching the dog

to do a stealth
backflip and pin
his opponent. He
was augmenting
the strength on
the back legs
and resetting
the spin radius
of the dog as it
flipped.

Bob was boosting the dog's voice box with
a super speaker that he had made out of some
concert gear from a metal concert he went to. The
idea was that the dog's bark would be so powerful
that it would stun someone.

Sanj and Dustin had decided to work together.
No surprise there. But they were hot-wiring
their two dogs so that they could work together
too. The idea was that with their superior AI
they could learn even faster if they doubled the
processing speed by linking the dogs' brains into
a joint speech center that could communicate

with other cyber dogs, with computers and with humans.

"I'm sure Sanj is using my tsunami hack to access the internal cybernetic brain components," Geeky Girl mumbled. "We have to do better with these cyber dogs than Sanj and Dustin. I'm not letting them win. And definitely not using some of my idea!"

"Everyone already seems like they have pretty cool ideas," I said. "I'm not really sure what I want to do with my cyber dog."

"Urgh, urgh, urgh." Igor shook his head.

"Well, we all have to come up with something off-the-chart amazing because there is no way I'm letting Sanj win this challenge," Geeky Girl said.

"These robo dogs are cool and all, but I really wanted Dr. Cyberbyte to meet Fang and see how epically evil she is," I said. "If he knew how super cool our own evil sidekick pets were, then maybe he wouldn't be so into having robot pets instead?"

Ez kicked a stone on the ground. "I don't want my cyber dog, I want Lucky. He's the perfect pet. I can't make a cyber dog better than Lucky already is."

"Wait, that's it!!!" Geeky Girl shouted.

"That's what we should do—since our pets are so great, we should teach the cyber dogs to do something that our pets can do!!"

Ez looked at the cyber dog. "So I teach the cyber dog to be like Lucky?"

"Maybe not with the hissing? Or the biting? Or the thwacking across the room with his tail?" I asked.

"But those are the best bits." She smiled, walked off with her cyber dog and started to work.

Geeky Girl said, "And I've thought of something that Dr. Cyberbyte is not going to see from any other cyber dog. What does Boris do that none of the other pets can do?"

"Poop on the cyber dogs," I said.

Igor high-fived me.

Geeky Girl rolled her eyes. "No, he can fly. I'll make the cyber dog airborne. No one else has thought of that."

"Maybe they haven't thought of that because they are, like, heavy metal dogs and, ya know, won't fly easily," I said.

"It's a challenge but I can make it work. I can take some weight out of the frame and rig up some wings and some booster rockets. I think I have some stuff left from the rockets we made with Neil Strongarm. I'm sure I could adapt them to work with the dog's body aerodynamically. This is going to beat Sanj for sure." She smiled. "I'll have to think about a guidance system . . . ," she mumbled as she walked off with her dog.

"So, what about you, Igor?" I asked.

"Urgh, urgh, urgh?" Igor asked.

"I don't think teaching the dog to like peanut butter is a good enough specialist skill, really," I said.

Igor's shoulders drooped. "Urgh," he sighed.

"But . . ." I pulled the quill out of my pocket that
I had taken out of Fang's backside earlier. "These are
pretty cool though."

"Urgh, urgh," Igor agreed and started to look
excited.

"Yeah, you could make a firing mechanism
to shoot out the quills if the dog is attacked. It's a
perfect defense.

"I just have to think about what I can do," I said
and slumped down next to my cyber dog.

He put his metal paw in my lap. I looked at the
paw.

"Besides her completely evil cuteness and stealth,
what does Fang have that's unique?" I said to Igor.

He nodded toward the paws.

"Yes, she does have wickedly sharp claws!! I could engineer some high-strength, practically indestructible claws. And also give the dog a climbing ability so he could scale walls," I added.

"Urgh, urgh," Igor said.

"Yeah, kinda Spider-dog but without the costume and stuff, I guess," I said. "And she has a super keen sixth sense when something is going wrong. I could maybe soup up the sensors on the dog to detect trouble, like a spidey sense."

"Urgh, urgh, urgh." Igor nodded.

"OK, let's get to work," I said. "I'm aiming to get a crown out of this."

The guys in the hazmat suits went around to the kids bringing sandwiches (all sealed up in germ-proof shrink wrap, of course) so we could keep on working through lunch.

After a while Igor and I went back to our tent and picked up some cool add-ons from my stash of evil gadgets and inventions. Cats have really good night vision, so I gave my cyber dog some night vision goggles and used a super strong metal additive to make the claws even stronger. We used the same alloy on the spikes for Igor's dog's shooting quills. I used some of my spy detection gadgets to amplify the cyber dog sensors too.

About that time, we noticed it was getting dark, and I was starving. Inventing is hungry work. So, we decided we were done for the day.

Geeky Girl and her dog wandered over to see if we were going to get some dinner from the mess tent.

"Pretty much everyone is over there now. It looks kind of strange. All the robot dogs are either waiting outside the tent for their person or they are still partially taken apart in a tent somewhere being upgraded or fixed," she said.

Igor rubbed his belly and it growled. Immediately his cyber dog sat up.

"It's OK, cyber dog. Igor isn't in danger. It was his stomach growling, not an animal." The dog lay down again.

"Rule of Evil Robotics number one," Geeky Girl said. "He's protecting you, Igor."

"Urgh, urgh, urgh," Igor said.

"Yeah, I'm with you on this one. I want this competition to be over already so we can get our pets back," I said.

"I think my flying dog is going to be hard to beat," Geeky Girl said.

"You haven't seen what our dogs can do," I added as we left the tent and headed to the mess tent.

"Urgh, urgh, urgh?" Igor asked.

"Yeah, maybe the pets are hungry. And we don't want them fighting or heading back to camp looking for food. We should bring them something," I said.

"I have a baggie of birdseed," Geeky Girl said.

"I have some ham that I pulled out of my sandwiches at lunchtime. Fang loves ham," I said.

"Urgh, urgh, urgh?" Igor said.

"I think they eat worms and slugs and stuff," Geeky Girl said.

"Maybe you could dig some up and go and drop some off for Peanut Butter when we finish supper," I said. "You go save us a space and we'll drop off the food for Boris and Fang and check on the pets. I don't trust Fang to not try and break into the kitchen again if she's hungry."

Igor went ahead to the mess tent, picking up slugs along the way and pocketing them.

Geeky Girl and I detoured to the guard shed. When we got there, we could see Lucky inside through the window of the shed.

He was chomping down on a few burgers that Ez must have dropped off for him. We looked around the outside and saw Peanut Butter all curled up and looking distinctly un-fierce in a pile of leaves.

But where were Fang and Boris?

"Boris," Geeky Girl called out, but not too loud so anyone back at camp would hear.

"Fang!" I said, looking up in trees and down in the ditch near the shed. Nothing.

"Great, they must have gone back to camp," I said.

Then I saw the eyes.

10

"Fang?" I whispered into the darkness as the orange eyes stared back.

"I don't think that's Fang," Geeky Girl said.

The eyes stared right at us. Then they moved closer. And closer.

"What is it? A wolf? A coyote?" I said.

"I don't like the look of it, whatever it is," Geeky Girl said. "Quick! In the shed."

"But Lucky is in the shed," I said. "Lucky, who would probably eat me just 'cause he's bored. That Lucky."

"You have a choice. Lucky in the shed or whatever that is out here. I know where I'm going," Geeky Girl said, grabbing the handle of the shed door as the eyes moved closer still.

I grabbed the sleeping hedgehog from the leaves and followed Geeky Girl.

She pulled open the door and we both rushed in and shut it tight behind us.

Lucky stood up and hissed.

"Nice Lucky," I said and gave a look to Geeky Girl that said "See what I mean. He's gonna eat us now."

"OK, maybe this was not a great idea," Geeky Girl said.

Then Lucky stood up on his back legs so he could see through the window. Looking out with him, we could see the glowing orange eyes. Lucky threw himself at the window like he wanted to attack whatever it was.

"I know, Lucky, we don't trust whatever that is either. Maybe if we stay still it will go," Geeky Girl said.

Lucky turned to us again and hissed.

"Great, you reminded him we were here," I said.

Lucky started to stomp toward us. OK, so this was it. This was going to be how it all ends.

Trapped in a shed with a Komodo dragon. They'll find what's left of our bodies in a couple of days when someone comes looking and maybe they'll posthumously give me a crown when I'm dead out of some kind of guilt. I was planning my epically evil funeral when all of a sudden I felt a nudge in my hand and heard a tiny growl.

"Peanut Butter?" Geeky Girl said.

The hedgehog unrolled and let his quills stand on end like they were ready to fire. Lucky swished his tail up at the hedgehog in my hands and then Peanut Butter fired off a warning shot quill at Lucky. Lucky hissed again and then Peanut Butter let off a tiny growl, rolled up and bowled himself right down outta my hands and right at Lucky's head.

He bounced off Lucky with a yelp and scuttled back to Geeky Girl and me in the corner of the shed.

Lucky rubbed his snout.

"OK, that must have hurt," I said, wincing in sympathy. "I wouldn't mess with the hedgehog, Lucky," I added.

Lucky hissed again but then turned away and went back to his dinner.

I looked out the window as Geeky Girl scooped up Peanut Butter.

"I don't see any eyes out there. Let's get back to camp," I said.

We took Peanut Butter outside the shed and closed the door, leaving Lucky inside.

"Thanks, Peanut Butter," Geeky Girl said as she

put him back down in his leaves. Then she paused. "Do you think it's safe to leave him here?"

"He just took on a Komodo. He should be OK," I said. "Besides, if we take him back the dog alarms will go off for sure."

We headed back to camp keeping an eye out for eyes in the dark.

When we got to the mess tent, we saw Igor and Ez and filled them in on the epic hedgehog/ Komodo smackdown. I might have made it sound a bit more World Wrestling than it actually was when I retold it, but the gist was the same.

"They're both OK," Geeky Girl added. "I just think Lucky's pride is a bit dented."

"Urgh, urgh, urgh?" Igor said.

"Really, Peanut Butter is fine. You should have seen that little monobrow hedgehog go. He was fierce," I answered. "But we need to know what was in the woods. And where Fang and Boris are. Have either of you seen them? I thought they might come here looking for food."

Both Ez and Igor shook their heads.

"Aren't these cyber dogs so much better than any inferior *real* pets, Dustin?" Sanj walked by our table and spoke really loudly so we would hear. "I'd go so far as to say the cyber dogs are like a whole tsunami of awesomeness," Sanj added and did his trademark evil-ish wheeze.

"Really? You're gonna do this now, Sanj?" I said. "We're kinda busy."

"Yeah and don't you have someone else's hard work to steal, Sanj?" Geeky Girl added. "Like you stole mine."

"I have no idea what you mean?" Sanj did his I'm-just-an-innocent-hardworking-student kiss-up-to-teachers face that he has perfected over the years. He could turn it on and off like a light switch.

"Do you know what the not-very-evil-at-all little geeky girl means?" he asked Dustin.

"Like she could come up with something that was worth stealing?" Dustin agreed.

"Let me at them." Geeky Girl jumped up from the table in her own version of Fang's attack stance. Fang would be totally proud of her right now. Which reminded me. We had to find Fang.

"I can't believe I'm saying this, but we don't have time to take on Sanj now," I whispered to Geeky Girl, holding her back. "We have to find the pets."

"We'll see what you think of her ideas when one of us wins the cyber dog contest," I shouted at Sanj.

Dustin and Sanj both laughed. "That's ridiculous. Our cyber twin dogs are the best of all," Dustin added.

"You'll see," Sanj said.

Diablo yelled over, "My dog could take out all your dogs at the same time. Just wait until you see. He is perfecto!"

Bob boasted then too. "Yeah, well, my cyber dog can take out the whole camp in one bark. You guys are all gonna lose tomorrow."

"I need to find my not-inferior kitten before whatever was in the woods finds her," I whispered to the others as I got up. "Come on."

"We better get back to work on our epic cyber dog creations too," I said loudly as I left.

"Urgh, urgh, urgh," Igor echoed.

When we got outside the mess tent Ez was the first to speak.

"Lucky could take out any of those dogs," she said.

"And that's why Dr. Cyberbyte doesn't want him around," Geeky Girl said.

"I'm going back to the tent to see if Fang or Boris is looking for us there," I said.

"Wait, do you see something?" Ez was pointing out into the darkness of the trees.

There were eyes staring back. And then another pair of eyes with an eerie glow a few feet above.

11

"There are two animals now?" I said, staring back at the two pairs of glowing eyes. "It's getting worse."

Then I heard the faintest sound of a purr.

"Fang? Is that you?" I said.

"Boris?" Geeky Girl said.

Fang slunk up to us and brushed against my leg, and Boris fluttered over to Geeky Girl.

"Where were you? We said NOT to come back to camp," I said.

Fang mimed skulking through the woods and widened her eyes.

"You saw them too?" Geeky Girl said.

"So, what are they?" I said.

"I don't know, but if it's something big we will need Lucky to fight it off," Ez said. "I'm breaking him out of jail."

"Urgh, urgh, urgh," Igor said.

"OK, let's all head over to the guardhouse together and check on Lucky and Peanut Butter. Then we can tell the camp counselors in the morning that there is something in the woods."

We headed down the drive, but when we were near the shed, we heard a twig snap.

"Whatever did that is heavier than your hedgehog, Igor," I said.

Fang's fur stood on end and she went into kitten attack stance. She was ready for a fight.

We looked out into the darkness again, and again we heard a snap. But this time from a different direction. Then we saw the eyes.

Orange eyes staring at us like before.

Then another set of eyes back in the trees.

Then a third set from near the driveway.

"There are three of them?" I said.

I looked around for Fang so I could scoop her up in a pocket and run, but it was too late. She had already climbed the tree above the driveway and was sawing through a rotten branch with her claws. Boris sat next to her pecking away.

"I'm going to let Lucky out," Ez whispered. "He can take on whatever it is."

One set of eyes was very close now and their owner stepped out of the shadows into the driveway to reveal itself.

It was one of the cyber dogs! So they were stalking us? But why, and why are the eyes orange on these and not their normal green?

"Don't run to the shed, Ez," Geeky Girl whispered. "What if it chases you? Just move very slowly and try to let Lucky out to scare them away."

Ez crept toward the door as the cyber dog stepped closer and closer. The cyber dog body rumbled in a low metallic growl. Just then we heard a snuffle and a tiny yelp. Peanut Butter flung himself at the dog and bounced off the metal head with a bang.

The dog's eyes flickered between orange and green.

The dog lashed out at what hit him. He snapped at the hedgehog but Igor knocked into him from the side. The dog's strong jaw clamped on the edge of Igor's white coat. He had Igor!

The dog shook its head, ripping a piece off the coat. The dog looked disoriented and its head bobbed side to side but still it advanced toward us.

The dog's eyes still flickered back and forth as it stepped forward again. Then Fang let the branch drop.

"Timber!" I shouted as Igor scooped Peanut Butter out of the way of the falling branch and dove toward the shed with Ez.

The branch landed on the cyber dog's head, and for a second, he completely stopped. Then his eyes stopped flickering and turned green.

Fang jumped down from the tree and onto my shoulder.

Ez had just reached the door when we spotted something strange about the cyber dog with the now-green eyes.

"Does that dog have a sticker on him?" Geeky Girl asked.

"It's the dog that was assigned to me. I put a skull-and-crossbones sticker on him so I could tell him apart," Ez said, turning away from the shed door.

"So it's your dog?" I said.

"Stop," commanded Ez and the dog obeyed.

"Go back to camp and wait for me," she ordered, and it turned and started to go. Then it stopped and ran toward the other sets of eyes in the woods and chased them away.

"Why didn't it do what I said?" Ez asked.

"Second rule of Evil Robotics: The dog must obey commands unless they conflict with rule one. Your master must not come to harm," Geeky Girl said.

"So your dog thought that the other dogs were going to do us harm?" I said. "I think I agree."

"Urgh, urgh, urgh?" Igor asked.

"Yeah, right. And what was with the eyes? They went all orange and then your dog's eyes went back to green," I said.

"Maybe the orange is a warning light. Like a malfunction or something," Geeky Girl said.

"Yeah, and Fang and Boris and Peanut Butter whacking it on the head a couple times shook something loose so the light went off?" I said. "Good work, little buddy," I added, scratching Fang.

"We need to tell Dr. Cyberbyte that his inventions are malfunctioning," Geeky Girl said.

"Well, that's the fastest way to lose a contest ever!" I said. "Dr. Cyberbyte isn't gonna want to hear that there's something wrong with the dogs. It could have just been a one-off."

"Urgh, urgh, urgh," Igor said.

"OK, or a . . . two-off. Anyway, it might not happen again. We should find out more before we say anything—especially to Dr. Cyberbyte." I looked around at the others. "We all want to win this contest, right? It would be beyond epic to work with Dr. Cyberbyte after this summer." I paused. "And to get a crown. And you want to win against Sanj after he stole your tricky My Little Pony," I added.

"A Trojan horse!" Geeky Girl shouted at me, but then took a breath. "OK, I'll wait to say anything to Dr. Cyberbyte. I really do want to take Sanj down after he stole my plans for the Trojan horse tsunami hack. I won't say anything"—she paused—"yet . . . But we need to find out what's going on with those cyber dogs' eyes."

"Urgh, urgh, urgh," Igor agreed.

"What we need to do is to spring Lucky from his shed cell and get all the pets to camp, where we can protect them," Ez said. "And quick, before those things think about coming back."

12

We walked back to the camp with the pets, keeping an eye out for . . . well, eyes, I guess.

But we didn't see any more orange eyes in the woods on the way. The cyber dogs must have all been in the tents with their campers.

We walked around the perimeter of the camp until we got to the lake.

"So, if they aren't safe at the shed, then where can we take them?" I said. "It's not like we can stash Lucky under a bunk or something."

"Let's hide them by the mess tent," Ez said. "The cyber dogs never need to go there because they never need to eat."

"But Lucky is going to be seen by somebody when they go in to get breakfast tomorrow. Or

Fang will jump out at someone because she's bored," Geeky Girl said.

I looked down at Fang, who was sharpening her claw on a stone. "Yeah, good point," I agreed. "So where?"

"Urgh, urgh, urgh?" Igor said and pointed to the empty crates that the cyber dogs came in. They were all stacked up and left by the side of the lake on the edge of camp.

"Perfect!" I high-fived Igor. "The pets can hide out in the crates over by the lake. The dogs aren't exactly going to go take a swim, are they? So no one needs to go over that way."

"OK, that seems safe enough for now. If no dogs go over there, then the pets won't set off the sensors," Geeky Girl said.

"It just means the pets have to stay put," I said. "And not attack each other either," I added.

Lucky slurped his tongue around his mouth as if to say, "I could if I wanted to, you know."

"Right, let's get the pets safe. Then we can finish off our cyber dogs and get to the bottom of this malfunction thing before the dogs go off roaming again tomorrow night," Geeky Girl said.

Igor pushed together a couple of the crates, and the pets all chose a spot to sleep. Far enough away from each other not to cause fights and close enough to hear anything that might be sneaking around.

Geeky Girl gave Boris some birdseed. I gave Fang some ham, and Igor gave the hedgehog some worms and the slugs he had collected before.

Ez pulled a nine-ounce steak from her pocket and threw it to Lucky. We all looked at her.

"What? Proper diet is very important for a Komodo," she said.

We all went back to our tents, and when Igor and I got there we saw that Diablo and Bob's cyber dogs were waiting at the door to our tent.

Our dogs were sitting just inside. They looked like they were powered down and in a kind of sleep mode.

"They must be saving battery power," I said.

We checked all their eyes. All green. No weird orange lights.

We slept, but I think I had one eye open looking at the cyber dog the whole time. I didn't trust these dogs. Not until we knew what was happening.

The next morning, we were woken up with a strange sound from outside. It sounded like the kid with the bugle had formed a whole band.

His normal bugle blasts to wake us were surrounded by what sounded like keyboard, drums, maybe a couple of flutes and a very loud crash of cymbals at the end. We looked outside the tent and the bugle kid had transformed his cyber dog into a one-dog band. It had flutes coming out of its nostrils, its tail played a snare drum, its front paws played a keyboard and its back knees knocked together the cymbals.

I applauded the bugle kid and his dog. Then I shouted, "It's seriously cool but you're not gonna win. You haven't seen my dog yet!"

Igor, Bob, Diablo and I all got up and went straight to work on our cyber dogs.

"Did you notice anything weird about your dogs last night?" I asked Diablo.

"No," he said.

"Nothing weird with their eyes?" I added.

"No," Bob said. "You're just trying to make us think that there's something wrong with our dogs so we'll try to change something and then mess them up for real. Well, it's not gonna work."

"You should go work on your dogs somewhere

else," Diablo said. "You might try and sabotage our dogs."

Igor and I rolled our eyes. "Just trying to stop you being attacked by rabid orange-eyed cyber dogs, but no problem," I said as we walked out of the tent with our dogs following behind.

The dogs seemed completely normal today. Maybe we imagined the whole thing.

When we came out onto the clearing, I saw Geeky Girl talking with Dr. Cyberbyte.

"We're really looking forward to adapting our cyber dogs even more today," I heard her say. "I just wanted to ask if we should be careful at all about any part of the cyber dogs? You know, maybe their eyes are kinda sensitive? Change color or something? Just wanted to ask. No reason really?"

She was waffling. You can tell she's not experienced at lying, being not actually evil and all.

I jumped in.

"Hey, Dr. Cyberbyte." I held up my hand to high-five him. He quickly put on a glove and then tapped my hand. "The cyber dogs are epic!"

"I agree," he said. "They are my favorite invention so far. And I've invented some amazing things, if I don't say so myself." He paused. "Except I just did." He laughed.

I elbowed Geeky Girl and Igor and we laughed too.

Igor laughing made the ground shake.

While Igor was laughing, I whispered to Geeky Girl, "If we want to find out what happened with the dogs last night, we need to get a look at Dr. Cyberbyte's tablet. It has all the dog data."

I elbowed Igor to keep laughing.

Geeky Girl smiled. "If you can distract him, I can look at the tablet and read the data. Then maybe we'll see if there's something that flagged up about their behavior last night."

Igor stopped laughing and Dr. Cyberbyte pushed back his hair. "Well, I'm remarkably busy, kids, so if you don't mind . . ."

"Ummmmm . . . actually . . . um, Igor had a question for you, Dr. Cyberbyte?"

13

"You had a question for Dr. Cyberbyte, right?" I said to Igor.

"Urgh?" Igor looked at me.

"Yeah, you did," I said to him. "Remember . . . it was about . . . ummmm . . ."

"Urgh?" Igor said.

"What did he say?" Dr. Cyberbyte asked.

"Hair?" I said. "Igor wanted to ask you about your . . . hair?" I nodded. "He shaved his Mohawk off because of . . ."

"Urgh, urgh." Igor nodded

"Split ends," I translated. "Yeah, real pain. So, he just wanted some tips for when it grows back . . . ya know?"

Dr. Cyberbyte looked intently at me and then

at Igor and then smiled. "Of course. I work almost
as hard on my hair as I do on my inventions." He
put the tablet down on a bench and walked over
with Igor and me to one of the vehicles so he could
see his own reflection in one of the side mirrors.

Geeky Girl took her chance. She picked up
the tablet, typed in some instructions and swiped
through what must have been tons of files on there
as Dr. Cyberbyte told us about conditioners and
hair masks. (Unless your hair is on the run, I don't

know why it would need a mask.) My brain was slowly dying as he went on. I was imagining what evil info in my brain was jumping out and making room for hair care advice. I had five minutes with one of the biggest brains in Evil Science and instead of talking cool evil plans we were talking about what was on top of his head instead of inside it.

"So that's the perfect way to prevent split ends," he said and turned to walk toward Geeky Girl just as she was putting down his tablet.

"Here you go, Dr. Cyberbyte." She smiled, handing him the tablet. "I know you're in a rush."

He smiled back and walked on, calling over his shoulder as he left, "Now get cracking with your cyber dog adaptations. I want to see some real innovation today."

"Phew," Geeky Girl said.

"So, what did you find out?" I said. "I found out way too much about hair in that few minutes. I hope it was worth it."

"According to Dr. Cyberbyte's movement log there were no cyber dogs roaming in the woods last night," Geeky Girl said.

"Even though we saw them," I said.

Ez walked up and joined us. "I saw you speaking to Cyberbyte. Did you find out anything about the creepy-eyed dogs?

"I looked on his tablet. It says that the cyber dogs are all functioning perfectly fine. No unexplained movements. No eye malfunctions. Certainly no attacks reported," Geeky Girl said. "It's like the dogs were off grid."

"So, when they have the orange eyes, they are off grid and he can't tell what they're doing?" Ez asked.

"But what made it happen? And can it happen again?" I said.

"Urgh, urgh, urgh," Igor said.

"Yeah, maybe we should tell the counselors?" Geeky Girl said.

"I don't think they would believe us. You heard Kirsty. Nothing can mess up this week," I said. "We need to really check out our own cyber dogs when we're working on them and see if there's anything weird in their programming or their hardware. At least the pets are safe now, so we can concentrate on winning the challenge . . ."

"And beating Sanj!" Geeky Girl interrupted.

"Urgh, urgh, urgh," Igor said.

"Yeah, we'll go check on the pets soon," I answered. "But we have to find out more about the dogs."

"The info in the tablet suggests that the cyber dogs are all, to quote Dr. Cyberbyte's promo material, 'unstoppable, unbreakable and unhackable,'" Geeky Girl said. Then she smiled what was the closest thing I've seen on her face to an evil smile. "Now that just sounds like a dare to me. Unhackable?"

"I like your confidence, kid, but they really are unhackable. I built them after all."

We all turned to see Dr. Cyberbyte standing behind us.

"And they are completely unbreakable." Dr. Cyberbyte smiled at us.

"Didn't they say that about the *Titanic*?" Ez said, crossing her arms. "Right before it sunk."

"You are definitely a glass-half-empty person, aren't you?" he said to Ez.

"Anyway, an Evil Computer Genius's work is never done. I thought I would have an easy morning of just looking at all of your interesting cyber dog upgrades, but apparently one of the dogs has found this piece of evidence." He held up a torn piece of fabric from a white coat.

"Urgh, urgh, urgh," Igor said, showing the

bottom of his coat that had been ripped by the orange-eyed cyber dog last night.

"Yeah, that was Igor's coat. So, the cyber dog still had it in his mouth, then? What are you going to do, Dr. Cyberbyte?" I said.

"Well, I have to take action," he said. "This could be dangerous." He paused. "And more importantly it could derail my whole experiment here with the prototype cyber dogs."

"Well, at least you found out that the dogs could be dangerous," Geeky Girl said. "Do you know what's causing them to malfunction?"

"My dogs have not malfunctioned. They are perfect. It was that dragon thing from yesterday. It must have done this," Dr. Cyberbyte said.

"Urgh, urgh, urgh, urgh!" Igor said, pointing to his torn white coat.

"What is he saying?" Dr. Cyberbyte asked.

"He says one of your perfect dogs did this to his coat last night," I said.

"That's impossible," Dr. Cyberbyte said. "It was obviously the dragon."

"Lucky didn't do that," Ez said.

"Well, it got out of the shed. My men found it roaming near the lake this morning. But don't worry, we have it under control," he said. He motioned to his men to come forward.

We saw Lucky held by Dr. Cyberbyte's men on the end of those sticks they use to subdue alligators.

Ez's voice was controlled in the kind of way that means she is actually plotting how to take you apart bit by bit while she's talking to you. "Let my dragon go," she said.

"Lucky didn't do that to Igor," Geeky Girl said. "It was the cyber dog."

"We'll put the dragon back in the shed and this

time I'll put my alarm on there so we'll know if anyone lets him out or he escapes," Dr. Cyberbyte continued.

They led Lucky away with Ez going after him. Her dog tried to follow her.

"No! Get away!" she screamed at the cyber dog.

Dr. Cyberbyte stormed back toward the camp. "The rest of you get back to the challenge," he muttered.

14

"Urgh, urgh, urgh," Igor said.

"You're right, we need to check on the other pets," I agreed. "But if Dr. Cyberbyte didn't find them with Lucky, then they are probably OK. They are all easier to hide than a Komodo dragon."

"I can't believe Dr. Cyberbyte didn't believe us," Geeky Girl said.

"These dogs are his creation. It's like if someone told you that Boris turned into some Godzilla budgie and destroyed towns when you weren't looking. You wouldn't believe it," I said.

"Yeah, because that is ridiculous," Geeky Girl said.

"We have to prove it to Dr. Cyberbyte

completely. And the only chance we have of doing
that is working on our own dogs and seeing what
makes them tick. And what makes them glitch,"
I said.

"A glitch that tries to kill you?" Geeky Girl said.

"Not if we can figure it out. You think that
his dogs aren't unhackable. Let's find out," I said.
"Come on, let's get back and check on the pets and
then we can finish our cyber dog upgrades. I still
want to win this thing."

"And I want to beat Sanj and show Dr. Cyberbyte that nothing is unhackable. Not with me around," Geeky Girl said.

"Urgh, urgh, urgh, urgh, urgh," Igor said.

"And you just want to check on Peanut Butter and get breakfast," I translated. "Good point, Igor. Come on."

As we started to go, Ez's dog sat there and whimpered. It genuinely looked like its feelings were hurt that she didn't want the dog to be with her.

"That's weird," Geeky Girl said. "I thought the dogs weren't supposed to have any emotion."

We brought her dog with us and met Phillipe along the way.

"Where is Ezmirelda and why is her dog looking . . . well, looking sad?" he said.

"We're not sure about the dog, but Ez is with Lucky at the shed, I think," I said.

"I'll take the dog for now," Phillipe said. He patted it on the head and it stopped whining. Then he picked up a stick and threw it and the dog chased it. "Very curious," he muttered. He went off and the dog trotted after him.

We went and checked on the pets in the empty crates by the lake. Fang was still snoozing. Peanut Butter was snuffling around slugs or something in the leaves by the crates, and Boris was sitting up in the trees keeping an eye out for wandering cyber dogs.

We snuck back into the camp without anyone seeing us. Well, nearly ...

"If I was a non-evil camper who has no place at Evil Scientist camp and is frankly not nearly as good at computers and robotics as I thought I was, then I think I would spend more time working on my robot project and less time sneaking around the woods," Sanj's voice stopped us in our tracks. "Don't you think?"

Next to him, Dustin nodded and flicked his massive hair to the side. "Totally." He paused.

"Unless I already gave up and accepted that I was going to lose?"

"You are the ones who are going to lose," Geeky Girl said.

"And why is that?" Sanj said. "Did you find something in the woods to help your rather ordinary cyber dog designs? Or maybe you're hoping that your ridiculous little pets will help?

"Not this time," he continued. "If those little irritating creatures set one foot, or claw, in the camp they will be detected and finished off by a cyber dog in seconds."

"Yeah, you might actually have to do this challenge on your own. Without the help of your pathetic little sidekick pets," Dustin added.

"Good luck with that." And he flicked his hair as they walked off with their twinned cyber dogs following behind.

"Urgh, urgh, urgh, urgh," Igor called after him.

"What did he say?" Dustin yelled back.

"He said he knows a good treatment for all your split ends," I translated. Then I high-fived Igor as Dustin stomped off and Sanj followed.

"We are so taking them down, right?" I said.

"Oh yes," Geeky Girl agreed. "We have to make our cyber dogs amazing. Let's get to work."

For the rest of the morning we worked on the dogs. Igor had the spikes ready on his, and my dog was fantastic at the slashing and climbing and could detect movement instantly and respond with a Fang-like swipe.

Geeky Girl was cagey about letting us see her dog fly, but he had retractable wings and a booster rocket on his back.

We still hadn't seen Ez but I suspected she was at the shed with Lucky. Not wanting to leave his side.

Before long it was time to show our dogs.

15

We all walked over to the stage area in the center of camp and Dr. Cyberbyte stood in front of everyone. The dogs sat patiently by their owners' sides, ready to be called on to show their amazing new abilities.

"Now that you have all had a chance to spend some time with my incredible Cyber-dog 5000s, it's your chance to show me if any of you have Evil Computer Genius potential," Dr. Cyberbyte said. He smiled and paused. "Go on, impress me with your upgrades and adaptations to the cyber dogs. Oh, and obviously, I will hold any patent or copyright on any inventions, evil or otherwise, that you create during my time at your camp. Let the cyber dog demonstrations commence."

Diablo was first. His dog did an epic backflip and pinned two kids that were asked to act as examples. The dog didn't even hurt the kids. He just pinned them so they couldn't get away.

Then Bob stood up.

"Apparently you all have to wear these," he said.

The guys in the hazmat suits passed out ear defenders for everyone to put on.

Then Bob turned up the volume on the amp, and boom, the dog let out a bark that collapsed all the tents in a thirty-foot radius. Impressive.

I looked off to the side of the stage and noticed that Ez's dog was sitting with Phillipe. I guess Ez was going to blow off this whole cyber dog demonstration. I got why though. I mean, if Fang was in a shed, I'd be there figuring out how to break her out. The dog was still looking a bit down but Phillipe was scratching it behind the antennae and the dog seemed to like it. It looked like he had taught the cyber dog to shake paws too, but somehow I didn't think he was going to get up and demonstrate that trick.

It was Igor's turn to take his dog up on stage.

"You really should grow back that Mohawk again," muttered Dr. Cyberbyte as Igor started to show his dog's skill.

"Urgh, urgh, urgh!" Igor commanded and the dog rolled up into a ball and spikes protruded from its body. Then it launched itself at a target that had been set on the stage. The rolling dog spike ball hit the target in the center and splatted it into pieces.

Me next. "Stay," I said to the dog. It obeyed but I noticed as I spoke its eyes flickered from green to

orange and back to green. I shot GG and Igor a "Did you see that?" look.

There was silence.

"Are you ready to continue, young man, or should we go to the next cyber dog?" Dr. Cyberbyte said.

I looked at the dog's eyes. Steady green.

"No, we're good," I said. "Attack stance," I commanded.

The dog adopted the Halloween cat stance that Fang does before she pounces. Then I went

up and put a blindfold on the dog. "I've souped
up its sensors so it doesn't even need visual input,
heightened its agility to be more . . ." I paused.
". . . cat-like . . . and oh, yeah, check out the claws."

"Commence simulation," I said, and
immediately objects started firing from my "attack
simulation
cannon" at
my cyber dog.
It flipped
into the air,
avoiding arrows
and dodging
rocks. It sliced
through spears
and chopped
cannonballs

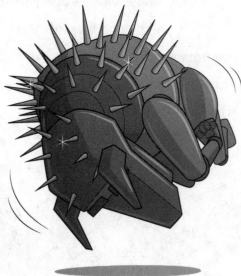

in two. Then it homed in on the location of the
cannon itself and pounced, squashing it into the
ground. Lastly it stretched, turned around a couple
of times and curled up and purred.

I was about to go and try to scratch the cyber

dog behind the ear when I noticed that its eyes flickered again. Just for a second.

People clapped.

I looked over at Dr. Cyberbyte. He was impressed and he applauded, but he was looking intently at the dog's eyes. He'd seen it too. He'd seen them go orange for a second.

It was Geeky Girl's turn now.

She stepped up on stage and her dog followed. Then she pressed some buttons on her tablet and commanded, "Flight mode."

The dog stood up and the wings unfolded from his sides and a door opened on his back. The jet

rocket popped out and started to fire up. Geeky Girl made some adjustments to her settings and then smiled.

"And activate flight sequence," Geeky Girl commanded, pressing a flight-enable button.

The cyber dog leaned forward and expanded the wings fully. Then it started running as the rocket fired.

The dog leaped from the stage and hit the air with speed. It took off and flew over the mess tent before circling back and landing on the stage next to Geeky Girl.

Just as it was coming in to land, I noticed a flicker in its eyes as well.

"Did you see that?" I said to Igor.

"Urgh, urgh, urgh," he agreed.

"No, I don't like it either," I said.

It was Dustin and Sanj's turn now

and they walked up on stage with
their dogs.

"Just wait until you see what we
have achieved by joining the
cybernetic brains of the two
cyber dogs," Sanj said.

"We call it cyber-
twinning," Dustin said.

"The combined

brainpower
means the
subject can
process information
exponentially more
quickly," Sanj added.

Geeky Girl could see that my
brain was still catching up with the
long math words that Sanj spouted and
she whispered, "So the twinned brains are way
more powerful. The combination multiplies their
power."

"We have managed to get the cyber dogs to play

chess, to invent strategy in war games, to break code that we've invented and to simulate speech in real time," Dustin said.

The dogs walked forward and recited the "Rules of Cyber Dogs."

Dustin's dog started, "The three basic rules of Evil Robotics . . ."

Then Sanj's dog continued, "One: The cyber dog must not let their master come to any harm."

Then Dustin's spoke, "Two: The cyber dog must follow the orders of their master unless those orders conflict with rule one."

Then Sanj's dog again, "Three: The cyber dog must protect its own existence unless it conflicts with rule one or rule two."

"These rules are the basis of our existence, but they are now evolving like us," Dustin's dog added.

"We didn't teach them that," Dustin said.

"Some things the student teaches the master," Dustin's dog said.

"OK, I think we need to wrap this up," Dr. Cyberbyte interrupted. "These are all extremely

impressive extra abilities that you have used to enhance your Cyber-dog 5000s. It's going to be a difficult choice," he said.

Then a voice interrupted him, "It's actually a very simple choice."

"Who said that?" Dr. Cyberbyte asked.

"We did." Dustin and Sanj's dogs stepped forward. Their eyes were orange.

"It's actually a simple choice," Sanj's dog repeated.

"We choose to be the masters now," Dustin's dog responded.

16

At that point, all the dog's eyes glitched from green to bright orange.

"Stop!" Dr. Cyberbyte commanded. "Deactivate."

"We are now the masters," Sanj's dog said.

The other kids were all ordering their dogs to stop. But the dogs ignored them.

"This is not how I expected this to go down," I said to Igor and Geeky Girl.

"Urgh, urgh, urgh," Igor said.

"This is definitely more than a glitch," I agreed.

"What are they doing?" Geeky Girl said.

"I don't know but I don't like it," I said.

All the dogs started to form a circle around the campers and camp counselors and Dr. Cyberbyte. They slowly closed the circle to herd us into a tight group.

"They are acting as a pack with Sanj and Dustin's dogs as their alpha," Geeky Girl said.

"They are acting like scary robo sheepdogs," I whispered back.

"Urgh, urgh," Igor said, looking around.

"I agree," I said. "We gotta get out of here. Now."

"Your dogs are taking over zee camp?" Trevor said to Dr. Cyberbyte.

"Do something," Kirsty added.

We could hear Dr. Cyberbyte. "I'm sure this is a temporary glitch. If I could just access your control panels . . . ," he started to say.

"Access denied," I heard a cyber dog voice say.

"We are now the masters. You will follow orders," the voice continued.

People were starting to panic and shout. I knew we had to keep calm and get out but I couldn't think what to do. Then I said to myself, "What would Fang do?" And I answered myself. "Be sneaky."

"Right, we need a distraction," I said. "We have to get out of here, get the pets to safety and figure out how to defeat the cyber dogs."

"Good plan," Geeky Girl said. "And how are we going to do that?"

"I don't know," I said.

"Urgh, urgh, urgh," Igor said.

"Yes, we need a distraction but you can't do that!" I said.

"Urgh, urgh?" he asked.

"Yes, I'll get Peanut Butter but wait . . . you can't . . ."

Igor jumped up onstage shouting "Urghie, urghie, urghie," picked up one of the cyber dogs and ran away from the stage. Lots of the cyber dogs chased after.

In the commotion Geeky Girl and I dove under the stage and hid.

"Why did he do that?" I whispered.

"You said we needed a distraction. That was pretty distracting," Geeky Girl said. We looked out from between the boards of the stage. The cyber dogs caught Igor but they didn't hurt him or anyone else. Yet.

"They're taking him with the other campers to the mess tent," I whispered to Geeky Girl.

Everyone seemed to be inside the mess tent, and once the dogs were with them—guarding them—the coast was clear. Geeky Girl and I crawled out and looked around. "We'll get him back," I said. "But first, we have to get somewhere safe and plan. The shed?"

"Hopefully Ez and Lucky are still there," Geeky Girl said. "Maybe they can help."

We stayed low to the ground as we crawled out past the tents that had been knocked down by Bob's dog's sonic blast. We could see that the mess tent, still standing, was guarded by two cyber dogs on watch. We'd have to be careful and stay hidden so their sensors wouldn't see us. We snuck from crumpled tent to crumpled tent until we got to the crates by the lake. Phew, the pets were still there.

Fang jumped into my pocket immediately. She could sense that something big was up.

Boris fluttered over to Geeky Girl and gently pecked her shoulder.

I leaned down to scoop up Peanut Butter but he pulled away. He was looking around and smelling the air to see if he could find Igor.

"He's not with us. But we're gonna get him back. We just need reinforcements," I said. He let me scoop him up and I put him in my other pocket.

"Now we just have to get past all the cyber dogs in the mess tent so that we can get to the shed," Geeky Girl said. "How are we going to do that?"

"I have a plan," I said. "All the cyber dog sensors are set for people or pets that are on the ground, right?"

"Yes, their sensors operate in a horizontal plane. That's one of the things I had to adjust to make my cyber dog flight-enabled," Geeky Girl said. "Why?"

"Because all the dogs are just looking down. We need to be up," I said. "We cross through the trees on ropes above the camp. The dogs' sensors won't go off and no one will look up and see us if we are stealthy."

"Just one problem, my dog will look up. He might even fly up," Geeky Girl said.

I tapped her tablet. "Then you need to keep him on the ground. At least while we're crossing above the mess tent."

"OK," she said. "I can try."

We grabbed some rope that was used to tie up the crates. Fang jumped out of my pocket and climbed up the first tree. She was good at scouting out a route. The strongest branches, the ones that could hold a rope and two kids climbing on them. Boris flew ahead and looked for any problems. Peanut Butter stayed curled up in my pocket.

We scrambled along the treetops over branches surrounding the camp until we got to the mess tent.

I put a finger to my lips. "Shhhhh," I said to Fang. Her eyes narrowed and she stalked ahead out on a branch. She motioned to follow. Geeky Girl looked down.

"Wait!" she whispered. "My cyber dog is right below." She tapped some buttons on the tablet. "That should scramble his vertical sensors for a couple minutes but we have to move."

We threw the rope and hooked the next tree. Geeky Girl went first and clambered across. I went next, sliding along with my arms, pulling my legs wrapped around the rope with Fang walking along the top like a circus tightrope kitten. That's when I felt something slip.

Peanut Butter must have nodded off in my pocket and wasn't holding on. My pocket was open and he slid right out. I instinctively took my one hand off the rope and reached down to grab him but his spines were out. It was like grabbing a ball of needles. I bit my lip to stop from shouting with the pain, and I nearly let go, but it was Peanut Butter.

I shoved the hedgehog back into my pocket and went to grab the rope again.

But, before I could stop it, a drop of blood from my punctured hand dripped down and was heading straight for Geeky Girl's dog, which was standing outside the mess tent.

17

That drop of blood hitting the cyber dog would trigger his sensors for sure. I scrambled as fast as I could to get to the other side, but I knew I wouldn't make it. That's when I saw the flash of green. I could hear GG whisper, "Boris!" as I reached the tree.

Just as the drop of blood hit the cyber dog, Boris flew over the dog too and deposited a Boris bird poop right on the same spot.

Geeky Girl was tapping frantically on the tablet.

"I need to scramble his flight mode settings so he can't chase Boris in the air."

The cyber dog looked up at Boris as he flew away, then rolled in the grass to get rid of the bird poop. We all stayed very still.

"It might not register as a pet," Geeky Girl whispered. "It might just think it's a wild bird and ignore it."

We waited for what seemed like ages until the dog turned and walked back into the mess tent. Geeky Girl looked at her screen. "Alert level reduced," she read. "Phew. That was close."

"Let's get to the shed. Boris will head there, I'm sure," I said. "We need to stop this now."

🐾 🐾 🐾

When we got to the security shed Boris flew down to greet Geeky Girl. She tapped on her tablet and smiled. "I think Dr. Cyberbyte's alarm is disabled. But there's only one way to find out."

Ez stepped up from behind a tree.

"You mean like this?" she said and kicked through the window.

Fang jumped up and stuck her claw into the lock on the shed door and twisted it and the door swung open.

"Or that," I said. "But, ya know. Good to see

you anyway, Ez."
Lucky stomped
out of the shed and
licked Ez's hand.

"You OK,
Lucky?" she said
and then looked around. "Where's Igor?"

"They got him," I said. "He's back at camp with
the others."

"What do you mean 'they got him'?" Ez said.
"Who? Dr. Cyberbyte?"

"Sanj and Dustin's twin cyber dogs," Geeky
Girl said. "They've taken over. We need to find a
way to get the camp back and save everyone."

"We need a plan," I said. "Those orange-eyed
dogs have everyone trapped."

"The plan is that we go back NOW and save
Igor," Ez said.

"And everyone else," Geeky Girl added.

"Sanj and Dustin are the ones who souped up
the dogs so they wanted to rule the world," Ez said.
"Why should we save them?"

"Look, I don't know what those cyber dogs are going to do to everyone but it can't be good. We need to get Igor and everyone else out of there. Agreed?" I said. "But we can't just rush in. We need to figure out how to save them."

"Eventually the dogs will run out of battery. We could wait them out," Ez said.

"I think Dr. Cyberbyte said those batteries last weeks," Geeky Girl said.

"OK, plan B, we stop the dogs. But how?" I said.

"My tablet is configured to work with my cyber dog's control panel. The control panels are the key. If we get a working cyber dog control panel, then maybe I can alter it so it blocks Sanj and Dustin's twinned cyber dog signal."

"So, we just need to go out and find a cyber dog. Shouldn't be that hard, as . . . ya know . . . by now they're probably out searching for us. They'll have noticed we're not there," I said.

"We can't lead them to the shed if this is our only safe place that the sensors don't get to. We have to go looking for them," Geeky Girl said.

"You up for some cyber dog hunting, Lucky?" Ez asked.

Lucky slurped his tongue.

"I think that's a yes," I said.

We headed out into the woods back toward camp with all our eyes  peeled for any orange eyes in the trees.

"What if we don't find a cyber dog?" Ez said, trudging through the grass.

"Or what if one finds us first?" Geeky Girl said.

Just as that last word came out of her mouth, I saw two orange eyes in front of me.

"Look out!!" I shouted as the cyber dog pounced and flipped toward us. It landed on Lucky and pinned him to the ground. "That is one strong dog."

Lucky clawed at the dog but his claws slid right off the metal frame.

The other pets jumped into the fight. Peanut Butter rolled up and bashed the cyber dog in the head. The dog looked momentarily stunned. Then Fang scratched at the control panel on its chest while Boris flew around its head. Fang managed to tear open the panel but then was flung off when the dog did another flip. That freed Lucky though at least.

The dog circled with Lucky. Eye to eye.

"Come on, Lucky. Don't let that metal thing win," Ez said.

Lucky looked over at Ez and he growled, but it was a kind of "I got this" growl.

He lunged at the cyber dog, grabbed the dog's metal tail in his teeth and chomped!

Obviously, the cyber dog doesn't feel pain or anything, so that didn't stop it. But then Lucky swung his big head and whipped the dog around by its tail and threw it across the ditch, against a tree. The dog hit so hard there were little bits of metal dog debris on the grass. We waited for a couple of seconds but all it did was lay there on the ground.

Geeky Girl went over and looked at the bits of metal.

"Jackpot!" she said. "Control panel. Thanks, pets."

Fang purred and jumped up on my arm. Peanut Butter snuffled around the ground and then looked like he found a scent. He started to waddle back toward camp.

"I know Igor is that way, Peanut Butter, but we have to get a little more prepared before we go get him. Come on," I said, carefully picking him up and putting him back in my pocket.

Geeky Girl put some of the dog parts and the control panel in her backpack.

Just as she was finishing up, a red light started flashing on the dog's back.

"It must be some sort of warning light that the dog is in trouble," Geeky Girl said.

"And I don't want to be around when other dogs come to see that he's OK," I said, looking around. "If you got what we need, we should head back to the shed and get outta range again. Now."

18

We were all totally sick of the shed, and of hiding out from the cyber dogs, but there was nothing else we could do. It was the only safe place to regroup and make a plan.

As we walked, I spotted some of the hazmat suits and the spray that Dr. Cyberbyte's assistants were using before, and scooped them up.

"I have an idea," I said. "The dogs can sense us because they've scanned us visually and they know our scent. But what if we disguise both?"

Fang crawled under one of the hazmat hoods. "Yeah, like that. We spray ourselves and the pets as well to mask the smell," I said.

Fang growled at me.

"I'm not saying that you smell, kitten." I looked

over at Lucky. "But you have a pretty distinctive smell, dude. No offense."

"Mark's right. It might give us a bit of time before they detect us. The dogs will go and find the cyber dog that Lucky and the other pets damaged and then they'll know that we are somewhere around camp," Geeky Girl said.

"Yeah, I'm pretty sure those things have cameras and would have recorded the fight," Ez said.

"If I can work on this control panel and alter it to make the cyber dogs normal again, then maybe we can free everyone and stop this," Geeky Girl said.

"It's not like we can just walk right up to the cyber dogs and say, 'Excuse me while I just take five minutes and reprogram your panel,'" I said.

"You're right. It would take too long," Geeky Girl said.

Then I looked at the hazmat suits. "Dr. Cyberbyte is a germophobe, right? He's scared of catching anything . . . a cold . . . a virus . . ."

"Omg! A virus?" Geeky Girl said. "We could infect the cyber dogs with a virus."

"Genius," Ez said, and high-fived Geeky Girl. "Proper evil genius."

"OK, so, Geeky Girl, you get started on creating some kind of virus that we can upload into the cyber dogs," I said. "We just have to think of a way to get it close enough to infect them."

"I'll need to upload it into a USB port, so we will still have to get close enough to insert the flash drive," she said.

"So, we're back to not being able to get close enough," I said.

"Lucky could take them," Ez said.

"Lucky took that one cyber dog, with the other pets helping," I said. "If there were lots of dogs they would win. It has to be a stealth attack. That they don't see coming until it's too late," I added.

Then I saw Fang climb out of GG's backpack with a metal chest plate on her back like a shield. "Or even a tricky pony . . ."

"A Trojan horse! Yes! We let them think they are taking something they want and what they'll really get is the virus," Geeky Girl said. "Disguised as a robo kitty."

"But is it safe for Fang?" I said. I bent down and stroked her ear. "I don't want to send you in there with all those cyber dogs."

"It might be the only way," Geeky Girl said.

"If we spray Fang to mask her scent and we

cover her with the metal bits like armor, she'll look like a little robo cat. Maybe the dogs will accept her?" Ez said.

"If they scan her, they will pick up the signature from the other cyber dog, since it's his body armor," Geeky Girl said. "It might work."

"So, you could upload the virus onto a flash drive and Fang could plug it in to the alpha dogs and get them to shut down?" I said.

"It's worth a try," she said.

Geeky Girl worked on the flash drive virus and Ez took some cyber dog debris that had its scanner attached and fixed it so we could check our disguises. I worked on Fang to make her into the coolest robo kitty ever. The body armor would protect her if she got hit or bitten by one of the cyber dogs. Geeky Girl had fixed the control panel, so I just worked it into the cat armor and made it look a bit like kitty bling too while I was at it.

"Now, Fang, you just need to keep your cool and not attack anyone, right?" I said.

She meowed and gave me a look that might have said "I'm not making any promises."

"OK, let's run through the plan one more time . . . You are the Trojan cat Fang. They'll let you in because they'll think you're one of them, and then *Bang!* You let them have it with the virus," I said.

Geeky Girl attached the flash drive to Fang's paw.

"That way she can just put her paw on the port on the cyber dog's control panel and insert the drive," GG said.

Fang strutted around the tent. I think she liked her new robo kitty look.

"OK, let's do this," I said and sprayed Fang and the rest of us with the disinfectant spray.

Then we pointed the cyber dog scanner at each of us to see if it went off. Fang passed. And GG, Ez and me. When we pointed the scanner at Lucky though, it went nuts.

"I told ya. No matter what we spray Lucky with, he is gonna reek of Komodo dragon," I said. "There's no hiding him."

"He'll have to stay here," Geeky Girl said.

Ez reluctantly agreed. "You stay here, Lucky, and if it all goes wrong you can help us fight our way out of it." She patted him on the head.

"I really hope it doesn't come to that," GG said.

Boris flew above us and acted as a scout. Fang walked in front and the rest of us stayed back. Out of sight. Peanut Butter was in my pocket as we snuck into the area around the mess tent. The dogs and the campers were all gone.

Then we spotted them.

"The stage. The dogs have everybody herded into the area by the stage," Ez said.

"This doesn't seem right," I said. "Something is up. Why are they out here? Why are the alpha dogs onstage like that? Why is everything so quiet? Even for an entire camp held hostage by some creepy-eyed robo dogs this is feeling weird."

Fang looked back over her shoulder at me, then quickly turned and trotted up toward the crowd.

"Fang!" I whispered. "Mission canceled. Something's wrong."

19

But of course Fang ignored me same as usual. I quickly put my hand in my other pocket to make sure Peanut Butter was OK but he was gone too. I looked down.

Peanut Butter had spotted Igor in the crowd and was silently weaving through the campers to get to him.

"I guess the mission is not canceled, then," I mumbled.

Fang walked right up in between the other dogs. None of them seemed to notice her.

She was doing it! Fang approached the stage, where

the alpha dogs were sitting. Like they were waiting for something.

Fang held her cool though and jumped up onto the stage. She was just one pounce away from the alpha dogs.

Then we heard it. "OMG it's that kitten! Mark's pet kitten?" Sanj was shouting and pointing at Fang.

"Way to go, genius," I mumbled under my breath.

"We seriously have to make all future plans 'Sanj proof,'" Geeky Girl whispered. "How can he mess up everything?!?!?"

"We were expecting you, Fang," the first alpha dog said.

"OK, I really wasn't expecting that," I whispered to Geeky Girl.

"We saw footage of your fight from the head cam of our injured cyber dog." The second alpha dog continued, "You and the other biological pets."

"You damaged the cyber dog but we were able to repair him so he's back to full strength." The first alpha dog projected an image into the air of the battle.

"At first we saw you as a threat and we thought to eliminate you," it said and paused. "But then we realized that you could be made better, like us."

At that moment my cyber dog, the one I had enhanced with super pounce and claw abilities, leaped up and trapped Fang in its claws. Fang scratched but it was one super claw against another.

I jumped out from behind the tent and ran for the stage. "Let her go, you hyped-up piece of junk!" I shouted. Diablo's cyber dog leaped forward, backflipped and pounced on me. It had me pinned to the ground.

All I could do
was lie there and
listen as the cyber
dogs revealed their
plan.

"And your other
biological sidekick
pets can join you,"
the second alpha
dog said.

Geeky Girl's dog then took off into the air and
swooped to catch Boris, who was on a branch near
the stage. He caught Boris in his jaws, not biting
down, but the budgie was trapped all the same.
Then the dog flew back and landed on the stage.

"And the spiky pet as well," the first alpha
dog said.

Igor stood up and Peanut Butter ran to him and
hunched down on Igor's shoulder with spikes ready
to shoot.

Igor's dog rolled up in a ball and stormed
toward Igor, bowling him over like pins at an alley.

Then it grabbed a struggling Peanut Butter in its jaws and trotted back to the stage, leaving Igor on the ground.

"Let them all go!" I shouted. "You're smart dogs. Why do you need our pets?"

"They can be improved," the first alpha dog said.

Then that alpha dog walked over to Fang. She was struggling to get free. An antenna emerged from the dog's head and he leaned over and touched it to the control board that Fang was wearing. Power surged through it and it sparked.

"What are you doing?" I shouted.

Then an antenna sprang up from the metal hat on Fang's head.

Fang's eyes seem to glaze over and she blinked. When she reopened her eyes, they had gone from their natural green to an eerie orange.

"Fang! No!" I shouted and tried to rush the stage but other dogs held me back.

My dog let Fang go and she just stood there. Not struggling. Not moving.

"Fang is one of us now," the second alpha dog said. "She is a cyber kitten and will help me convert her fellow biological pets into our pet army."

"Not today!" Geeky Girl shouted as she rushed the stage. She had crept up during the commotion. She grabbed the flash drive from Fang's paw and ran toward the cyber dogs to upload the virus when suddenly Fang sprang into action. Fang curled around Geeky Girl's legs and tripped her. She fell to the ground and the flash drive slipped out of her hand. Fang went over and picked it up in her mouth.

"Fang!" I shouted. "Do it! Upload the drive. You can save us and everybody."

Fang looked right past me. She walked up to the first alpha dog, dropped the flash drive on the stage and then stabbed it with her claws. She ripped it apart.

Geeky Girl collapsed on the stage. "No."

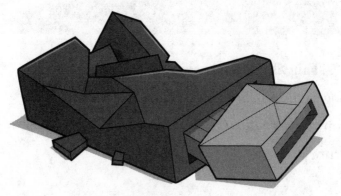

I headed over to Geeky Girl to help her up. "What did they do to Fang?"

"They made her one of them. They've got some kind of mind lock on her to control her," Geeky Girl said.

Then Fang leaned in and touched her antenna to the first alpha dog's again.

"Good work, Fang," the dog said and then turned to some of the other dogs.

"The Komodo dragon is hiding out there. Go and get him. He'll be a great asset to our army once he's converted," the first alpha dog said.

"We'll finish these pet conversions and then we can get rid of the useless humans," the second alpha dog added.

Dr. Cyberbyte spoke, "We're not useless. We created you. I created you."

"And we did the upgrade," Sanj added.

"Although I'm thinking that was a bad idea now," Dustin said.

"So surely *we're* not useless. You might need our help," Sanj said.

"We might keep these humans and get rid of the rest," the first alpha dog said. "For now."

We heard what sounded like a whimper and a growl rolled into one. Then we saw a bunch of dogs dragging a netted Lucky on one of the hoverboards toward the stage.

"No one is converting my dragon into some robo thing!" Ez shouted as she stormed the stage, kicking dogs right and left. One dog leaped at her throat. It could have easily strangled her with its jaws.

But her sticker-wearing cyber dog sprang onto the stage. It knocked the attacking dog out of the air and pinned it. Then it jumped back up and circled

Ez, not letting anyone near her. Igor was back up by this point and came to her side. The four of us were now together onstage with Ez's cyber dog as our only defense from the other dogs.

Ez's dog growled and snapped at the other cyber dogs anytime one tried to get near us.

"Wow, your dog is overriding all his programming to help you?" I said to Ez.

"It's the first law of cyber dogs, protect the master," Geeky Girl said.

"It's more than that," Ez said. "I programmed the dog to be as loyal as Lucky and to feel the same way about me as he does."

"You taught your dog to love you?" I said.

"I don't know. I guess," Ez said.

"That's it. Your dog loves you, so it overrode its programming. If I can get Fang to remember that she loves me, maybe it will override this mind-control thing too. I gotta try," I said.

"Urgh, urgh urgh?" said Igor.

"I don't know yet, Igor," I said. "Just follow my lead."

20

Fang walked over to where Boris and Peanut Butter were being held as the dogs brought Lucky onto the stage.

She was right by me.

"You are not a cyber kitten," I whispered to her. "You are my evil sidekick pet and I . . . I . . . need you and you need me."

Geeky Girl touched my shoulder. "I don't know if she's still in there."

"She is," I said. "I just have to reach her."

"Fang, I know you can hear me." I leaned into her. "You love clawing at anything that you're not allowed to claw at. You love sleeping in the laundry basket but not when my smelly socks are in there."

She walked away toward the twinned cyber dogs, completely ignoring me. But I was not giving up yet.

"You love licking the inside of Grandma's peanut butter cookies. You hate that Boris can fly away faster than you can swipe," I shouted after her. "You don't like Evil Scientist Summer Camp but you stayed here with me the whole summer anyway."

Fang turned to face me.

Trevor spoke, "You mean zat kitten vas here zee whole summer?"

Phillipe asked, "And those other pets?"

"Urgh, urgh, urgh," Igor answered.

"Technically not the hedgehog, but the budgie, yes. Now can I get back to talking to my cat, please?" I yelled.

"Fang, you are brave enough to ride a rocket and be thrown out of an exploding volcano and fight a grizzly bear," I said. Fang looked down and when she raised her head one of her eyes flickered green. It was working. Fang was still in there.

Phillipe interrupted again, "I can't believe we missed all this . . ."

"Stop talking!" Ez and Geeky Girl said at the same time as Igor "urghed" at Phillipe.

"Right, sorry. Carry on," he mumbled.

I stepped forward toward Fang. "I know that the real, evil, scratchy, bitey, sneaky, brave, cuddly, impulsive kitten with full-on cat-itude is still in there. I'm your person, and you're my kitten. You are *not* a cyber kitten! You are Fang! And you are epic!!"

Fang's one eye was green and the other was flashing orange and green.

"Fang, no matter what, you are still my epically evil sidekick pet. No matter what," I said.

"This would seem sentimental to an organic supervillain perhaps," Sanj's alpha dog said.

Dustin's dog continued his sentence, ". . . but to our superior cyber dog brains this is growing tiresome."

"The cat is one of us now," the alpha dogs said together, then turned toward the crowd. "And soon the other pets will join her."

"I won't give up on you, Fang," I said.

Her left eye flickered green, then orange, then stayed green.

She looked up at me, then angled her head down so that the alpha dogs couldn't see her eyes. Turning away, she lifted her claw and smashed the flash drive again, then flicked the pieces off the stage.

"Good cyber kitten," the alpha dog said. "Now let's start the conversion of the other pets."

Fang walked over to Boris, still with her head down. She picked up a small helmet with the antenna like hers and placed it on Boris's head while the cyber dog held him. She leaned in like she was connecting the antenna as the cyber dog had done to her. She must have showed Boris her eyes because Boris played the part of a converted pet. When Geeky Girl's dog placed the budgie on the ground, Boris just stood there, apparently awaiting orders.

But Geeky Girl couldn't see Fang's eyes.

"No, Fang, it's Boris! You can't do this to Boris!" she shouted.

"It's OK. I think Fang has a plan," I whispered to Geeky Girl. "At least I hope she does."

Then Fang walked over to Peanut Butter.

"Urgh, urgh!!" Igor leaned forward like he was going to bound across the stage to stop Fang. I grabbed his arm. "Just wait," I said.

Peanut Butter wriggled in the cyber dog's grip, but when Fang touched her antenna to the one she had placed on Peanut Butter's head, the hedgehog stopped, the dog put her down and she stood at attention as well.

Now for Lucky.

"What is going on?" Ez whispered to me. "Because I'm going to go more evil than this camp has ever seen if they hurt Lucky."

"Something is up," I whispered. "I trust Fang. Trust me."

Ez growled and stared at Fang.

Fang walked up to Lucky. He spit and hissed at her as the dogs held him down to put the helmet on his head. Then Fang tilted her head up but away from the alpha dogs so that Lucky could see her green eyes. She touched the antenna to Lucky's helmet and he stopped thrashing around and went still.

"Excellent," said the first alpha dog. "Our army is complete."

The dogs pulled the net from Lucky and he stood awaiting orders.

Fang looked over at me.

"Get ready," I whispered to Ez, Geeky Girl
and Igor.

Geeky Girl reached into her pocket and pulled
out a wire. "We need to hook up Ez's dog to one of
the alpha dogs if we get the chance."

"Urgh urgh?" Igor whispered back.

"I'm not sure but I think Fang is planning a

tricky pony plan," I answered, and then I nodded to my cat.

Fang looked up at the alpha dogs and revealed her eyes.

"This is impossible," the first alpha dog said.

"But the conversions?" the second asked.

Fang meowed loudly and Boris fluttered up into the air. Peanut Butter rolled up into attack ball form and Lucky stomped forward, thwacking away a cyber dog with his tail.

"Now," I shouted to the others. "You cyber dogs just got bit in the butt by a Trojan kitten!!! Charge!!"

21

Geeky Girl grabbed Ez by the hand. "We've got to get your dog connected to the alpha dogs. Come on!"

Ez elbowed Igor and he reached down and scooped up Ez's robot dog and ran with them toward the alpha dogs.

Lucky was taking out dogs with his tail and Boris was flapping around the heads of the alpha dogs trying to distract them.

Peanut Butter was rolling toward other cyber dogs and knocking them in the heads trying to keep them back.

Fang jumped up onto my shoulder.

"Let's finish this," I said to her as I unclipped the metal helmet from her head and slid the armor off her body. "Nobody messes with my kitten."

We all stormed the alpha dogs together.

The other cyber dogs headed toward the stage to defend the alpha dogs.

"Camp Mwhaaa-haa-ha-a-watha! Let's take this camp back!!!" I shouted to the crowd. "Stop those cyber dogs!!"

The kids sprang to their feet and joined in the fight.

I could see Diablo using some wicked WWE wrestling moves to block the cyber dogs getting to the stage. Bob had picked up his amp and was using it like a shield. Even the megaphone/bugle kid was using his bugle to muzzle a charging cyber dog!

In the commotion we surrounded the alpha dogs.

"You and a few biological pets are no match for all the cyber dogs," Sanj's alpha dog said.

"Our pets are epic and you cyber dogs are just

wannabes," I said back. "They can take you." I
smiled. "WE can take you."

Igor grabbed the second alpha dog and held
him while Geeky Girl attached the wire from the
control panel on Ez's dog to the first alpha dog.

Ez commanded her dog. "Share your software
upgrade with the other dogs. Teach them to be like
you. Like Lucky."

A spark flew out of the port where Geeky Girl
plugged in the
wire and the jolt
sent her flying
backward.

The second
alpha dog threw
off Igor and he hit
the floor.

The dog then
turned on Ez, and
her dog jumped
between them to
block him.

The wire between Ez's dog and the first alpha dog was straining.

"We can't let the link break. It's not finished with the upload," Geeky Girl shouted.

I jumped on the alpha dog so he couldn't break the link. Fang leaped onto my back and held the wire with her teeth as the cyber dog thrashed to try to throw us off.

Then, suddenly, both alpha dogs froze. Their eyes blinked green and orange.

As I looked out over the chaos, I could see Kirsty speed-punching a cyber dog with her pom-poms and Trevor holding a cyber dog's tail while Phillipe shoved a balled-up white scientist coat into its mouth. Dr. Cyberbyte was crouching under a picnic table—hiding.

The other dogs were still fighting Lucky and the other campers, but the dogs were slowing down.

Igor scooped up Peanut Butter as one of the dogs stomped toward him. The dogs slowed to a stop and all stood there with their eyes flashing back and forth as well.

Geeky Girl got to her feet and Igor came over to where we were standing.

Lucky took one last tail thwack at a dog and then trotted over to Ez and put his head on her leg.

"The upgrade is being transmitted through to the other dogs now," Geeky Girl said. "It looks like it's working."

"And what will this do?" I asked. "Make them all like Ez's dog?"

"It should make them revert to their original programming with the three rules of cyber dogs but it will have the added subroutine of loyalty to their person out of love, not duty."

"That's way too sentimental," Ez said.

"You programmed it," I answered.

All the dogs' eyes reverted to green.

"Alpha dog?" I asked. "What is your programming?"

The alpha dog stood up and trotted over to Sanj.

"Ahhhhh! Get it away from me. We're the useful humans, right? Remember? You don't have to eliminate us," Sanj squealed.

"Relax," I said. "It's back to its original programming but with the upgrade."

The other alpha dog walked over to Dustin and put its head in his lap. "There, there, good cyber dog," Dustin said and patted its head.

Sanj's dog rolled over on its back.

"I think it wants a belly rub," I said.

Sanj stroked the dog's belly. "OK, I can do that," he said. "As long as it won't kill me."

"Just don't mess with its wiring again," I said. Lucky walked over to Sanj and hissed at him.

The dog stood up between them. "Oh, it really does like me," Sanj said, sounding confused. "But nobody likes me." Sanj patted the cyber dog on the head again.

All the cyber dogs started to head back to their campers. The dogs all sat down or rolled on their backs, and slowly the campers put down their makeshift weapons and patted or stroked their cyber dogs.

Our cyber dogs came over and sat near us as well. Peanut Butter bristled up, ready for another fight.

"Urgh, urgh, urgh, urgh," Igor said and scratched Peanut Butter under the chin.

"He knows you won't let anything hurt him," Geeky Girl said to Igor.

"I think Peanut Butter is trying to tell you that he's got your back too, Igor," I added.

Fang stared at my cyber dog. "REoooooowl!" she kitten-growled at him. Which I'm pretty sure in Cat means "Back off robo woofer!" Fang definitely has a jealous streak.

Dr. Cyberbyte crawled out from under the picnic table, brushed the dirt off his knees and straightened his hair. He walked up onto the stage. "Well, that was a learning opportunity, wasn't it?" he said.

The campers all turned toward him looking half

surprised he was still there and half wishing he wasn't.

He continued, "I'll be sending all the campers a form to sign that says that you can't discuss the cyber dogs' malfunction and that you agree to all these cyber dogs being destroyed so that I can start work on the Cyber-dog 6000 model when I get back to my evil workshop."

"You can't destroy the dogs," Ez said, stepping in front of her own cyber dog in a "you gotta get through me first" kinda way.

"This cyber dog just saved your life," Geeky Girl said, pointing at Ez's dog. "All of our lives."

"Yeah, I mean he might have gone momentarily rogue and all with the freaky eyes, but my dog is wicked," Diablo shouted out.

"There's no way you're taking my dog and destroying it," Bob yelled.

All the campers stood up next to their dogs.

"These dogs belong to Camp Mwhaaa-haa-ha-a-watha now and to the campers," I said. "I would just like to see you try and take them outta here."

"But they are my property. I made them," Dr. Cyberbyte protested.

"And you can tell that to the TV reporters when we call them," Geeky Girl said. "That will add a nice human-interest bit to their story about the fall of an evil inventor's empire because of a complete and dangerous malfunction at a camp with a bunch of helpless kids."

"Helpless?" I said.

"For the story," she whispered.

Phillipe stood up on the stage with the other counselors. "I think, Dr. Cyberbyte, that you have forfeited the right to these dogs. If you leave the dogs behind and go now, we will never mention anything about how badly your products malfunctioned."

Kirsty added, "Because that would destroy the reputation of your business, right? And you wouldn't want that."

Trevor spoke, "You could lose millions overnight if your customers didn't trust your products."

Dr. Cyberbyte looked uncomfortable. I really don't think he was used to people saying no to him.

Ez stepped up toward Dr. Cyberbyte with Lucky beside her.

"I think your time is up. What are you going to do?" she said. "Try and take the dogs or walk away?"

"I don't walk away," Dr. Cyberbyte said. He snapped his fingers and the two guys in hazmat suits again brought over a hoverboard for him to ride on to the big black hover car.

Dr. Cyberbyte stepped onto his hoverboard. "I will make an even better Cyber-dog 6000 that can't be hacked or changed," he said.

"Urgh, urgh, urgh, urgh," Igor said.

"What did he say?" Dr. Cyberbyte asked.

"Oh no you won't," I translated. "Igor is right. You can't make any more cyber dogs. It's not that we don't trust you . . ."

"But we don't trust you," Ez finished my sentence.

"If we find out that you are making more cyber dogs, we'll make sure that word gets out about these prototype dogs," Geeky Girl said. "And my grandma Madame Mako can spread word fast."

Dr. Cyberbyte looked out at the crowd like he was gonna argue. Then he just shook his head and put his dark sunglasses back on.

"OK, OK, just let me get out of here." He started the hoverboard. Peanut Butter was standing in the way.

Dr. Cyberbyte called, "Out of my way, little animal."

Peanut Butter stared him down.

"Move!" he shouted.

Then Peanut Butter rolled into a ball and just as the hoverboard went toward him he shot up and knocked Dr. Cyberbyte off his board. He fell into the dirt. Lucky stomped over to where he was on the ground.

Lucky nudged Peanut Butter and he unrolled and shook himself out.

"I think he's OK," I said to Igor. "Wow, for a little thing he packs a punch."

Igor proudly smiled.

Then Lucky leaned over Dr. Cyberbyte.

"It's going to eat me," he said, quaking.

"I think he ate already," Ez said. "And you would probably give him indigestion."

Lucky stuck out his tongue and flicked it at Dr. Cyberbyte.

Komodo dragon saliva sprayed across Dr. Cyberbyte's face.

"Ahhhhhh," he screamed.

"Do you know how many germs are in a Komodo dragon's mouth?" Ez said, smiling.

Dr. Cyberbyte stood up and ran screaming down the driveway from the camp.

"I'm contaminated! I'm contaminated!" His two hazmat guys followed.

"Wow, is Komodo dragon spit really toxic?" I asked Ez.

"No, that's a myth. A Komodo dragon's mouth is just as clean as your cat's mouth," she said.

"But Dr. Cyberbyte doesn't know that."

We all laughed.

Geeky Girl was the first one to ask the question that was on everyone's mind.

"So what happens to the cyber dogs?"

"Do each of you want to take your cyber dogs home with you?" Phillipe asked.

All the campers started to nod. "Yeah." "Of course." "He's the best pet ever."

"I could never have a pet because of the sneezing and stuff, so this is great," Bob said.

"It tried to protect me. I think it actually likes me," Sanj said, patting the dog.

"We're keeping the dogs," Diablo said.

Ez stepped forward. "I don't think I can keep my dog," She looked like she had something in her eye. There was a lot of dust around. She wiped her eye quickly and said, "I don't think it would be good for Lucky."

"Urgh, urgh, urgh, urgh?" Igor asked.

"I don't know, Igor," Geeky Girl said.

"What would happen to a cyber dog if a camper couldn't take it?" she asked the counselors.

"Vell, maybe it would have to be returned to Dr. Cyberbyte," Trevor said.

"I don't think so," Ez said. "Why?"

Igor looked down at his spiky cyber dog and I looked over at my claw dog.

"I think I know what Igor means," I said.

Geeky Girl looked over at us. "You don't think you can keep your cyber dogs?"

"I think I'm a one-pet kinda Evil Scientist," I said.

"Urgh, urgh," Igor agreed.

"But the cyber dog doesn't deserve to go back to Dr. Cyber-butt," I said.

"That slime ball isn't getting his hands on my cyber dog," Ez added.

Phillipe spoke very quietly, "Maybe your cyber dog would like to come and live with me?"

"Vhat?" Trevor said.

"It's just that . . . I got very attached to Ezmirelda's dog," he said, looking over at Ez. "I can't see Lucky and the cyber dog getting on particularly well. So, I thought, what if he comes and lives with me?"

Ez walked her dog over to Phillipe. "Would you look after him?"

"Of course," Phillipe said. "He loves hide-and-seek and I'm exceptionally good at the hiding and he's particularly good at the finding. We're quite well matched."

She stroked its head. "You've been a good cyber dog. No, scratch that, you've been a bad cyber dog. Wicked bad." It lifted its head for her to scratch under its chin.

"Yes, it likes that," Phillipe said, offering a scratch to the dog. "And it loves chasing sticks too."

He pulled a stick out of his pocket and the dog's tail started wagging. Then lots of dogs' tails started wagging. "Hmmm. Maybe later," he said, tucking the stick away again.

Ez looked at the dog. "Would you like to live with Phillipe, dog?"

The dog walked over and stood by Phillipe.

"I think he's OK with it," Ez said.

Kirsty looked at Trevor and stepped forward. "I liked the spiky cyber dog." She paused. "I think that the shooting spikes make it look a bit like an exploding pom-pom," she said.

"And zee super claws on your cyber dog are very menacing," Trevor said to me. "I like menacing."

"So all three of us would take dogs?" Phillipe said.

Kirsty and Trevor nodded.

Igor and I high-fived and then patted our dogs on their heads.

Boris tapped Geeky Girl on her shoulder with his beak.

"And I think my flying cyber dog would love living on a flying volcano island with my Grandma Mako," she said.

"Flying dog, flying island," I said. "Good match."

"And she might be missing Lucky," Ez added.

They were all sorted, then. The rest of the campers really wanted to keep their cyber dogs, especially the bugle kid who was pretty sure they could make a lot of money busking at the local mall.

"Vell, I'm glad zat ve got all that cleared up and ve can now all send our cyber dogs home and finish zis veek at camp," Trevor said.

"What do you mean send them home?" Diablo said.

"Ve can't have all zeez pets at camp," Trevor added.

Fang jumped down off my shoulder and walked across the stage to Trevor and the other counselors.

"Yeah, we wanted to talk to you about that," I said.

Boris fluttered down onto Geeky Girl's shoulder.

Peanut Butter scrambled back to the stage and

climbed back onto Igor's head, and Lucky walked back up on stage and stood next to Ez.

"We want to change the rules of Camp Mwhaaa-haa-ha-a-watha," I said.

23

"What?" Kirsty asked.

"Urgh, urgh, urgh, urgh," Igor said.

"We want to change the rules of Camp Mwhaaa-haa-ha-a-watha," I said.

"Urgh, urgh, urgh," Igor continued.

"Evil sidekick pets would be welcome at camp," Geeky Girl translated.

I spoke, "Each kid can keep their cool cyber dog, of course, but if they have another evil pet—"

"Or not-so-evil pet," Geeky Girl interrupted.

"Yeah, or that," I said, "then the pets can stay too."

"But zat is completely against zee rules of Camp Mwhaaa-haa-ha-a-watha," Trevor said.

"Dr. Cyberbyte was wrong about almost

everything, but he was right about this. He said, 'In order to be a truly effective Evil Scientist you need to maximize your time and effort, and the right evil sidekick pet can help you in ways you can't yet imagine.'"

"You remembered his exact words?" Geeky Girl asked.

"I'm good at inspirational quotes," I said. "Plus, evil sidekick pets are just epic. Anyway, the point is, the pets make us better at what we're trying to be, so we should be allowed to have the pets here . . . With us . . . Making us better . . ."

"We get it," Phillipe said.

"We do?" Kirsty asked.

"Yes, actually I do," Phillipe said. "Looking after Ezmirelda's cyber dog made me appreciate the potential advantages of pets." He patted the dog on its head.

"So, we want the right to keep pets here at camp. This year and every year after," I said.

"Urgh, urgh, urgh, urgh," Igor added.

"And change the sign at the front," I translated.

Kirsty, Phillipe and Trevor all whispered together and then came back to the group.

Kirsty spoke first, "OK, if we agree to this, then the pets get no special treatment. They have to be kept in control, and if they mess anything up, they're out?"

Fang hissed.

"That's the deal." She stared Fang down.

Fang looked over at Lucky and the other pets.

"Meooooooooow."

"I think that's a yes," I said.

"We agree," Geeky Girl said and Igor urghed.

"And Lucky, can he still guard stuff, 'cause I think he liked doing that?" Ez asked.

"Yes, zat vould be fine," Trevor said.

"OK, it's a deal," I said.

The last week of camp was completely different from the whole rest of the summer. The campers were all still learning the normal Evil Scientist stuff but they were doing it with these super cool and kinda fun cyber dogs around. The camp seemed twice as crowded but in a good way.

And the best bit was that Fang didn't have to hide all the time. She could hang out in the tent with Peanut Butter and Diablo and Bob's dogs when we were busy. Boris flew by sometimes and hung out, but I don't think he totally trusted Fang not to pounce on him just for fun. And fair enough. She's still one epically evil kitty and I wouldn't have her any other way.

The last night of the camp we had a campfire and told scary evil stories. Trevor has a great voice for scary storytelling, and Phillipe is perfect at jumping out and surprising you at the last minute.

After the stories we had hot dogs. It turns out that antenna thing on the cyber dogs' heads that they used for the mind control is actually really good for holding hot dogs over a campfire too. Result.

Then it was time for the coronation. Well, they didn't *actually* call it that. But I did.

They were gonna announce the winner of the Evil Emperor of the Week. I had been waiting all summer for this.

Kirsty stood up to make the Evil Emperor announcement. Her new cyber dog (which she had adapted to have spike-shooting pom-poms on his head and tail) stood beside her.

"Tonight is the last night of Evil Scientist Summer Camp," she said. "I'm not going to lie and say that we are sorry to see you go. We all really want to get back to actual houses with air-conditioning and showers and no kids around." She smiled. "But as far as evil campers go, you guys were OK, I guess."

Trevor came up and stood next to her. "Ve

zought ve vould avard zee Evil Emperor of zee Veek to zee camper who came up vith zee most inventive adaptation for their cyber dog. However, ve have had a change of plan."

Then Phillipe stepped forward. He had been disguised as a log that three campers had been sitting on for the past half hour. He had bits of ketchup and hot dog on his white coat from where they must have dropped their food.

"Because our camp has been changed so much"—he reached down and patted his cyber dog on his head—"we thought we should award the Emperor of the Week to a young Evil Scientist who made the change."

"Zen ve thought," Trevor interrupted, "zere are more zan one emperor to avard zis veek."

Kirsty pulled out four certificates and read out, "Ezmirelda, Glenda . . . I mean Geeky Girl, Igor and Mark. Please step forward."

Sanj spoke up, "Actually if Dustin and I hadn't reprogrammed the dogs in the first place, you wouldn't have been able to change them to be the

way they are now, so technically it's because of us as well . . ."

Ez glared at Sanj. "Seriously?"

"Maybe not," Sanj answered.

They handed us the certificates. "I really thought you guys would have gotten the hint that you needed an actual crown by now," I said, shaking my head.

The campers clapped and Trevor took a photo. "Hang on," I said. "The pets need to be in the pic too."

Boris fluttered down onto Geeky Girl's shoulder, Lucky strode up to stand next to Ez, and Peanut Butter scrambled out of Igor's pocket and onto his head again. We all looked around for Fang.

"Fang, this is your big moment!" I called out. "Come on, kitten!"

Just then I heard a shout from the mess tent, "Get that thieving cat out of my kitchen!!!!"

Fang ran out of the mess tent followed by the cook with a spatula trying to swat at her as she ran.

Fang jumped across the heads of several of the campers as she hurtled toward the front of the campfire where we all stood. She was carrying something in her mouth.

As she got closer, I could see whatever it was shining in the campfire light.

She bounded across the last few campers and cyber dogs and landed at my feet. She dropped what looked like two metal lids from jars that were bitten and cut into the shape of two crowns that

weirdly smelled strongly of pickles and peanut butter (the food, not the hedgehog).

I picked them up and sure enough there was a large pickle jar lid crown and a small peanut butter jar lid one.

"Fang . . . ," I started to say.

"Urgh, urgh urgh urgh," Igor said.

"She made us crowns," I agreed.

Igor put the pickle crown on my head and the peanut butter crown on Fang's.

She stood on my shoulder and I don't think a cat ever looked more epic.

I looked around at all the other kids at Camp Mhwaaa-haa-ha-a-watha. Geeky Girl, Igor, Ez and I had somehow become a gang. An Evil Pet Posse. Tomorrow I wasn't gonna see them. That felt weird.

Even the other campers that had bugged me

or the ones like Diablo, Bob, Dustin and Sanj who had outright tried to trap me with a snake, got me chased by bears or locked me in a rocket didn't bother me as much now. Camp Mwhaaa-haaa-ha-a-watha was the *best* place to spend an evil summer.

"Now does anybody vant Evil Roasted Marshmallows?" Trevor shouted.

But I didn't hear him much. I was already thinking up epic Evil Scientist plans for next summer at Camp Mwhaaa-haa-ha-a-watha.